GOSCINNY AND UDERZO
PRESENT
An Asterix Adventure

ASTERIX
AND
CLEOPATRA

Written by RENÉ GOSCINNY *and Illustrated by* ALBERT UDERZO

Translated by Anthea Bell *and* Derek Hockridge

Asterix titles available now

1 Asterix the Gaul
2 Asterix and the Golden Sickle
3 Asterix and the Goths
4 Asterix the Gladiator
5 Asterix and the Banquet
6 Asterix and Cleopatra
7 Asterix and the Big Fight
8 Asterix in Britain
9 Asterix and the Normans
10 Asterix the Legionary
11 Asterix and the Chieftain's Shield
12 Asterix at the Olympic Games
13 Asterix and the Cauldron
14 Asterix in Spain
15 Asterix and the Roman Agent
16 Asterix in Switzerland
17 The Mansions of the Gods
18 Asterix and the Laurel Wreath
19 Asterix and the Soothsayer
20 Asterix in Corsica
21 Asterix and Caesar's Gift
22 Asterix and the Great Crossing
23 Obelix and Co.
24 Asterix in Belgium
25 Asterix and the Great Divide
26 Asterix and the Black Gold
27 Asterix and Son
28 Asterix and the Magic Carpet
29 Asterix and the Secret Weapon
30 Asterix and Obelix All at Sea
31 Asterix and the Actress
32 Asterix and the Class Act
33 Asterix and the Falling Sky

Asterix and the Vikings

Coming soon

Asterix versus Caesar
The Twelve Tasks of Asterix
Asterix Conquers America
Operation Getafix

Original title: *Astérix et Cléopatre*

Exclusive licensee: Orion Publishing Group
Translators: Anthea Bell and Derek Hockridge
Typography: Bryony Newhouse

This revised edition first published in 2004 by
Orion Books Ltd,
Orion House, 5 Upper Saint Martin's Lane,
London WC2H 9EA
An Hachette Livre UK Company

5 7 9 10 8 6 4

Printed in France by Qualibris

http://gb.asterix.com
www.orionbooks.co.uk

A CIP record for this book is available from the British Library

ISBN 978 0 7528 6606 2 (cased)
ISBN 978 0 7528 6607 9 (paperback)

Distributed in the United States of America by Sterling Publishing Co. Inc.
387 Park Avenue South, New York, NY 10016

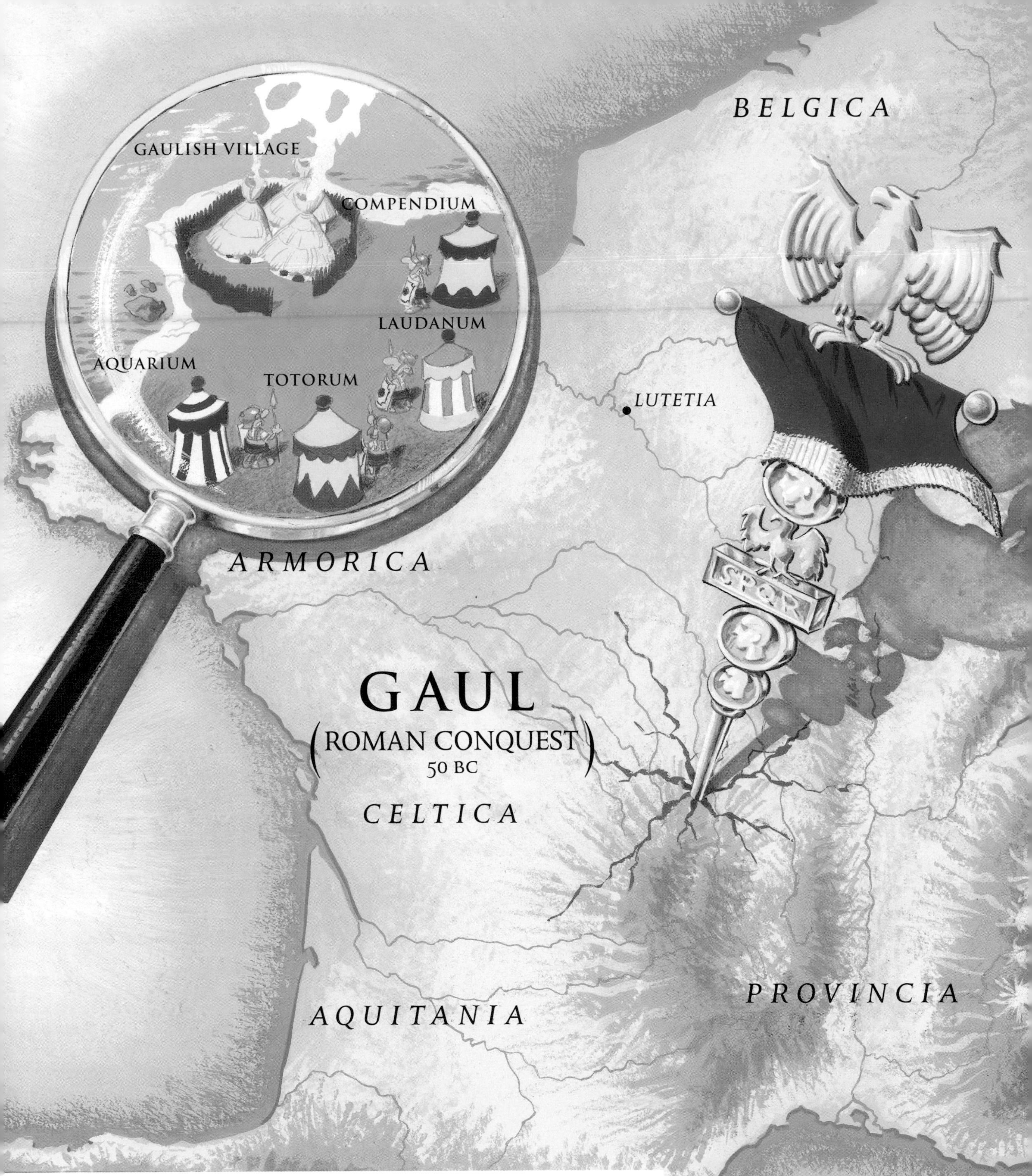
BELGICA
GAULISH VILLAGE
COMPENDIUM
LAUDANUM
AQUARIUM
TOTORUM
LUTETIA
SPQR
ARMORICA
GAUL
(ROMAN CONQUEST
50 BC)
CELTICA
PROVINCIA
AQUITANIA

THE YEAR IS 50 BC. GAUL IS ENTIRELY OCCUPIED BY THE ROMANS. WELL, NOT ENTIRELY ... ONE SMALL VILLAGE OF INDOMITABLE GAULS STILL HOLDS OUT AGAINST THE INVADERS. AND LIFE IS NOT EASY FOR THE ROMAN LEGIONARIES WHO GARRISON THE FORTIFIED CAMPS OF TOTORUM, AQUARIUM, LAUDANUM AND COMPENDIUM ...

ASTERIX, THE HERO OF THESE ADVENTURES. A SHREWD, CUNNING LITTLE WARRIOR, ALL PERILOUS MISSIONS ARE IMMEDIATELY ENTRUSTED TO HIM. ASTERIX GETS HIS SUPERHUMAN STRENGTH FROM THE MAGIC POTION BREWED BY THE DRUID GETAFIX . . .

OBELIX, ASTERIX'S INSEPARABLE FRIEND. A MENHIR DELIVERY MAN BY TRADE, ADDICTED TO WILD BOAR. OBELIX IS ALWAYS READY TO DROP EVERYTHING AND GO OFF ON A NEW ADVENTURE WITH ASTERIX – SO LONG AS THERE'S WILD BOAR TO EAT, AND PLENTY OF FIGHTING. HIS CONSTANT COMPANION IS DOGMATIX, THE ONLY KNOWN CANINE ECOLOGIST, WHO HOWLS WITH DESPAIR WHEN A TREE IS CUT DOWN.

GETAFIX, THE VENERABLE VILLAGE DRUID, GATHERS MISTLETOE AND BREWS MAGIC POTIONS. HIS SPECIALITY IS THE POTION WHICH GIVES THE DRINKER SUPERHUMAN STRENGTH. BUT GETAFIX ALSO HAS OTHER RECIPES UP HIS SLEEVE . . .

CACOFONIX, THE BARD. OPINION IS DIVIDED AS TO HIS MUSICAL GIFTS. CACOFONIX THINKS HE'S A GENIUS. EVERYONE ELSE THINKS HE'S UNSPEAKABLE. BUT SO LONG AS HE DOESN'T SPEAK, LET ALONE SING, EVERYBODY LIKES HIM . . .

FINALLY, VITALSTATISTIX, THE CHIEF OF THE TRIBE. MAJESTIC, BRAVE AND HOT-TEMPERED, THE OLD WARRIOR IS RESPECTED BY HIS MEN AND FEARED BY HIS ENEMIES. VITALSTATISTIX HIMSELF HAS ONLY ONE FEAR, HE IS AFRAID THE SKY MAY FALL ON HIS HEAD TOMORROW. BUT AS HE ALWAYS SAYS, TOMORROW NEVER COMES.

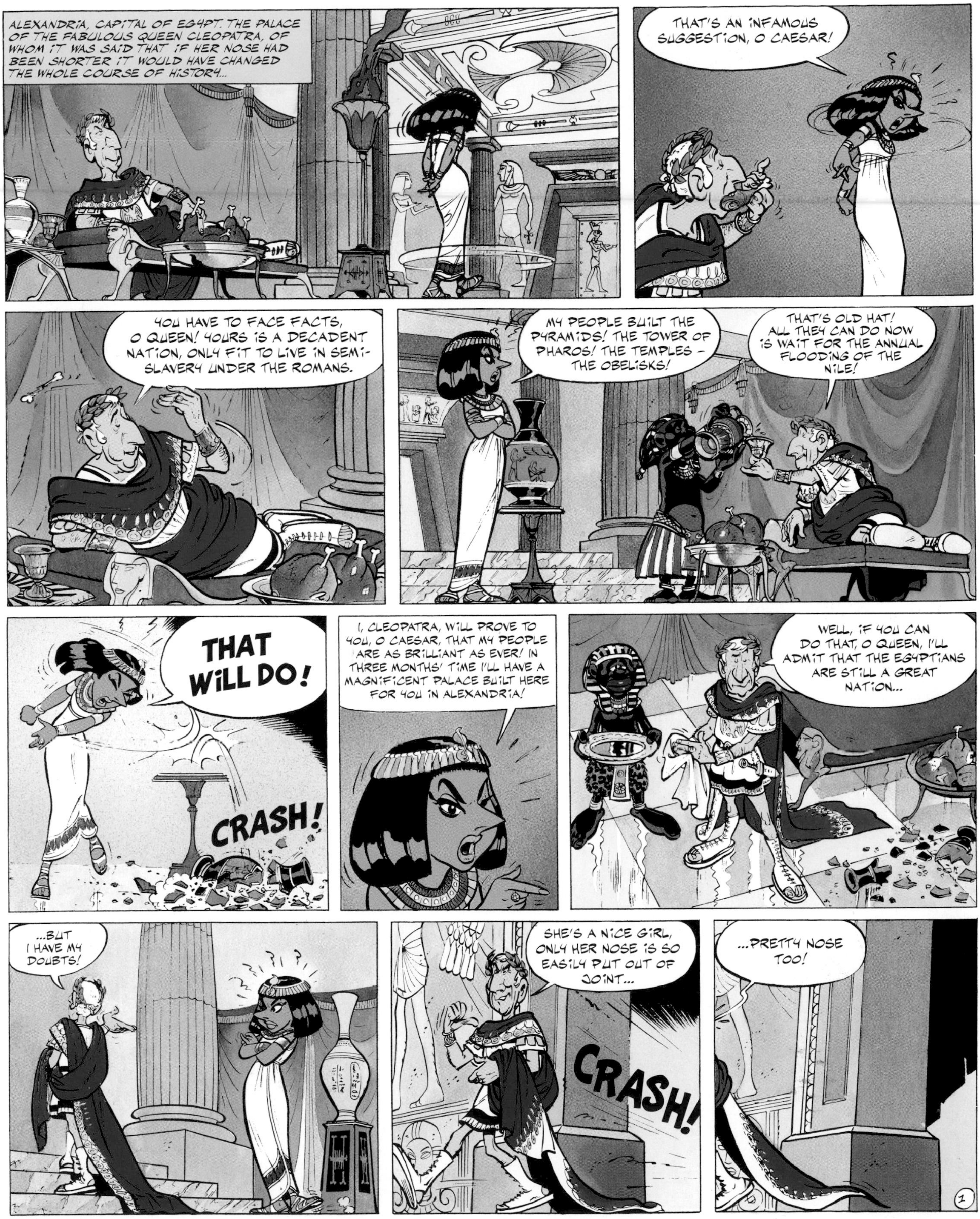

ALEXANDRIA, CAPITAL OF EGYPT. THE PALACE OF THE FABULOUS QUEEN CLEOPATRA, OF WHOM IT WAS SAID THAT IF HER NOSE HAD BEEN SHORTER IT WOULD HAVE CHANGED THE WHOLE COURSE OF HISTORY...
THAT'S AN INFAMOUS SUGGESTION, O CAESAR!
YOU HAVE TO FACE FACTS, O QUEEN! YOURS IS A DECADENT NATION, ONLY FIT TO LIVE IN SEMI-SLAVERY UNDER THE ROMANS.
MY PEOPLE BUILT THE PYRAMIDS! THE TOWER OF PHAROS! THE TEMPLES - THE OBELISKS!
THAT'S OLD HAT! ALL THEY CAN DO NOW IS WAIT FOR THE ANNUAL FLOODING OF THE NILE!
THAT WILL DO!
CRASH!
I, CLEOPATRA, WILL PROVE TO YOU, O CAESAR, THAT MY PEOPLE ARE AS BRILLIANT AS EVER! IN THREE MONTHS' TIME I'LL HAVE A MAGNIFICENT PALACE BUILT HERE FOR YOU IN ALEXANDRIA!
WELL, IF YOU CAN DO THAT, O QUEEN, I'LL ADMIT THAT THE EGYPTIANS ARE STILL A GREAT NATION...
...BUT I HAVE MY DOUBTS!
SHE'S A NICE GIRL, ONLY HER NOSE IS SO EASILY PUT OUT OF JOINT...
CRASH!
...PRETTY NOSE TOO!
1

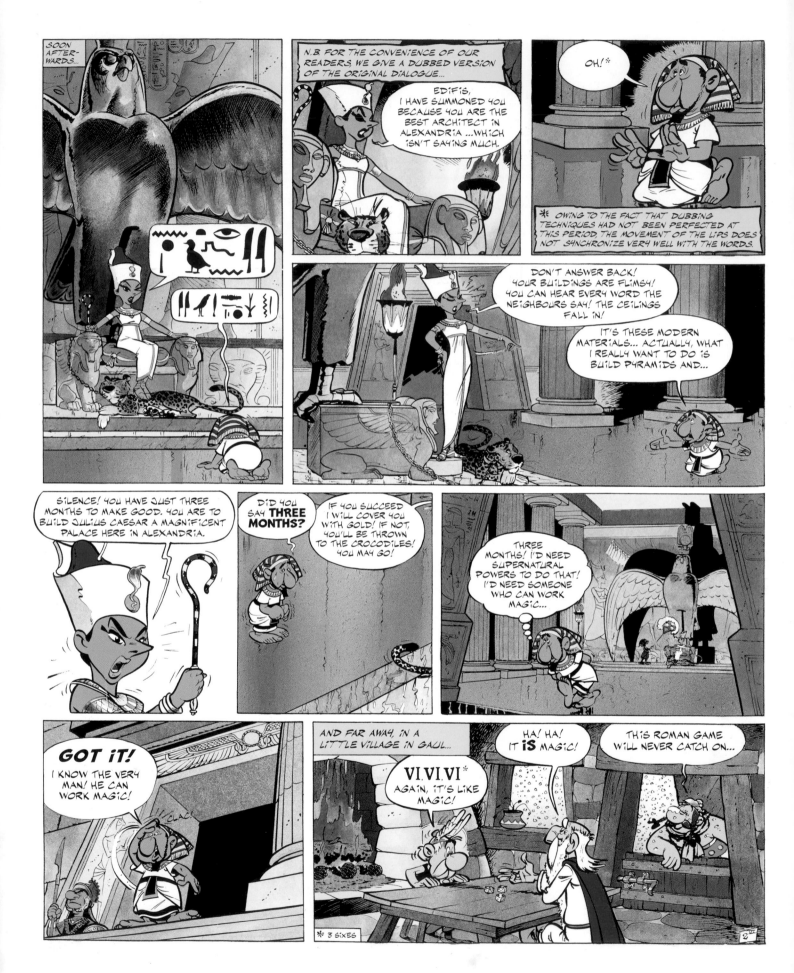

SOON AFTER-WARDS...

N.B. FOR THE CONVENIENCE OF OUR READERS WE GIVE A DUBBED VERSION OF THE ORIGINAL DIALOGUE...

EDIFIS, I HAVE SUMMONED YOU BECAUSE YOU ARE THE BEST ARCHITECT IN ALEXANDRIA ...WHICH ISN'T SAYING MUCH.

OH!*

* OWING TO THE FACT THAT DUBBING TECHNIQUES HAD NOT BEEN PERFECTED AT THIS PERIOD, THE MOVEMENT OF THE LIPS DOES NOT SYNCHRONIZE VERY WELL WITH THE WORDS.

DON'T ANSWER BACK! YOUR BUILDINGS ARE FLIMSY! YOU CAN HEAR EVERY WORD THE NEIGHBOURS SAY! THE CEILINGS FALL IN!

IT'S THESE MODERN MATERIALS... ACTUALLY, WHAT I REALLY WANT TO DO IS BUILD PYRAMIDS AND...

SILENCE! YOU HAVE JUST THREE MONTHS TO MAKE GOOD. YOU ARE TO BUILD JULIUS CAESAR A MAGNIFICENT PALACE HERE IN ALEXANDRIA.

DID YOU SAY **THREE** MONTHS?

IF YOU SUCCEED I WILL COVER YOU WITH GOLD! IF NOT, YOU'LL BE THROWN TO THE CROCODILES! YOU MAY GO!

THREE MONTHS! I'D NEED SUPERNATURAL POWERS TO DO THAT! I'D NEED SOMEONE WHO CAN WORK MAGIC...

GOT IT!
I KNOW THE VERY MAN! HE CAN WORK MAGIC!

CLAC!

AND FAR AWAY, IN A LITTLE VILLAGE IN GAUL...

VI.VI.VI* AGAIN, IT'S LIKE MAGIC!

HA! HA! IT **IS** MAGIC!

THIS ROMAN GAME WILL NEVER CATCH ON...

* 3 SIXES

6

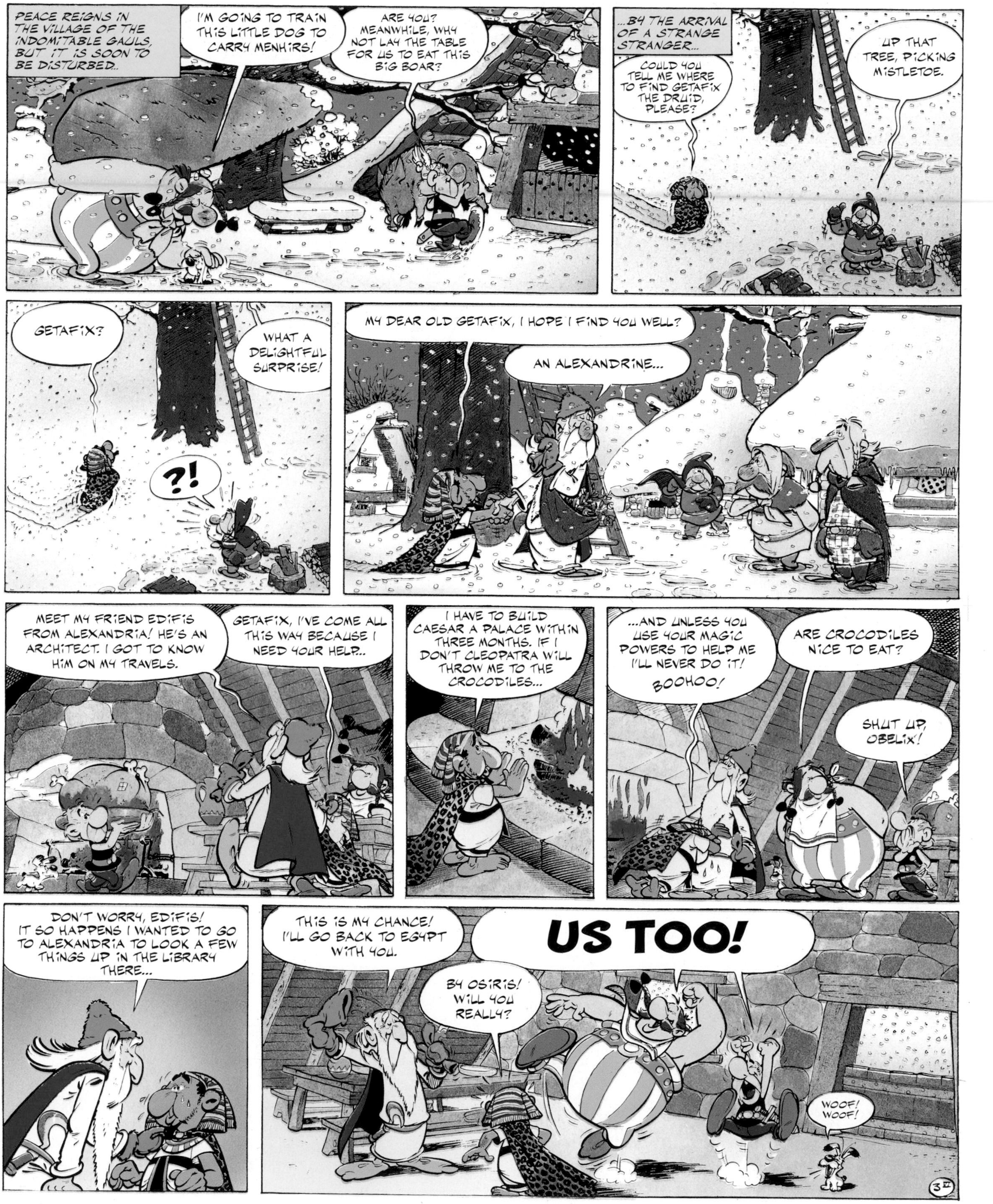
PEACE REIGNS IN THE VILLAGE OF THE INDOMITABLE GAULS, BUT IT IS SOON TO BE DISTURBED...
I'M GOING TO TRAIN THIS LITTLE DOG TO CARRY MENHIRS!
ARE YOU? MEANWHILE, WHY NOT LAY THE TABLE FOR US TO EAT THIS BIG BOAR?
...BY THE ARRIVAL OF A STRANGE STRANGER...
COULD YOU TELL ME WHERE TO FIND GETAFIX THE DRUID, PLEASE?
UP THAT TREE, PICKING MISTLETOE.
GETAFIX?
WHAT A DELIGHTFUL SURPRISE!
?!
MY DEAR OLD GETAFIX, I HOPE I FIND YOU WELL?
AN ALEXANDRINE...
MEET MY FRIEND EDIFIS FROM ALEXANDRIA! HE'S AN ARCHITECT. I GOT TO KNOW HIM ON MY TRAVELS.
GETAFIX, I'VE COME ALL THIS WAY BECAUSE I NEED YOUR HELP...
I HAVE TO BUILD CAESAR A PALACE WITHIN THREE MONTHS. IF I DON'T CLEOPATRA WILL THROW ME TO THE CROCODILES...
...AND UNLESS YOU USE YOUR MAGIC POWERS TO HELP ME I'LL NEVER DO IT! BOOHOO!
ARE CROCODILES NICE TO EAT?
SHUT UP, OBELIX!
DON'T WORRY, EDIFIS! IT SO HAPPENS I WANTED TO GO TO ALEXANDRIA TO LOOK A FEW THINGS UP IN THE LIBRARY THERE...
THIS IS MY CHANCE! I'LL GO BACK TO EGYPT WITH YOU.
US TOO!
BY OSIRIS! WILL YOU REALLY?
WOOF! WOOF!

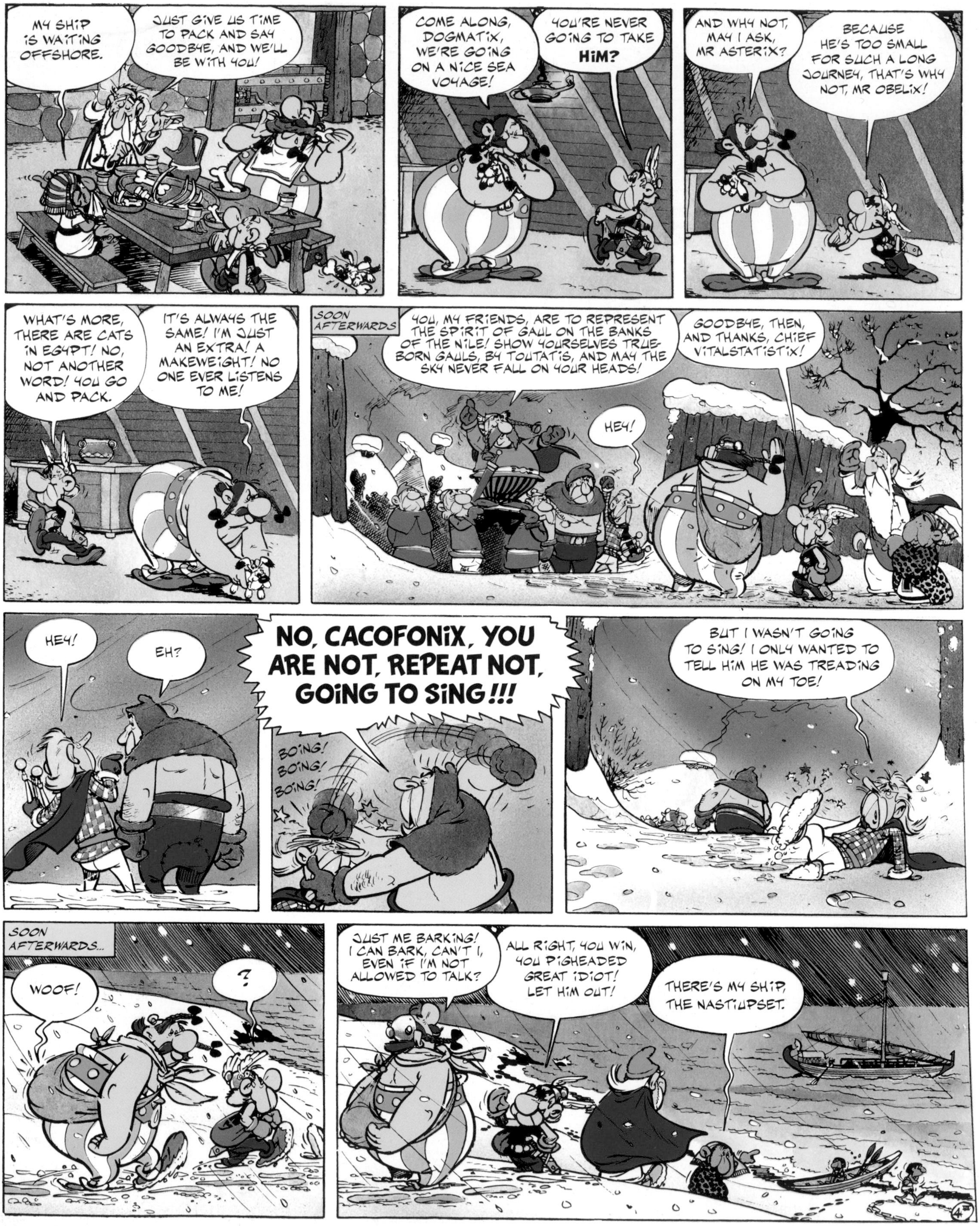
MY SHIP IS WAITING OFFSHORE.
JUST GIVE US TIME TO PACK AND SAY GOODBYE, AND WE'LL BE WITH YOU!
COME ALONG, DOGMATIX, WE'RE GOING ON A NICE SEA VOYAGE!
YOU'RE NEVER GOING TO TAKE HIM?
AND WHY NOT, MAY I ASK, MR ASTERIX?
BECAUSE HE'S TOO SMALL FOR SUCH A LONG JOURNEY, THAT'S WHY NOT, MR OBELIX!
WHAT'S MORE, THERE ARE CATS IN EGYPT! NO, NOT ANOTHER WORD! YOU GO AND PACK.
IT'S ALWAYS THE SAME! I'M JUST AN EXTRA! A MAKEWEIGHT! NO ONE EVER LISTENS TO ME!
SOON AFTERWARDS
YOU, MY FRIENDS, ARE TO REPRESENT THE SPIRIT OF GAUL ON THE BANKS OF THE NILE! SHOW YOURSELVES TRUE-BORN GAULS, BY TOUTATIS, AND MAY THE SKY NEVER FALL ON YOUR HEADS!
GOODBYE, THEN, AND THANKS, CHIEF VITALSTATISTIX!
HEY!
HEY!
EH?
NO, CACOFONIX, YOU ARE NOT, REPEAT NOT, GOING TO SING!!!
BOING! BOING! BOING!
BUT I WASN'T GOING TO SING! I ONLY WANTED TO TELL HIM HE WAS TREADING ON MY TOE!
SOON AFTERWARDS...
WOOF!
?
JUST ME BARKING! I CAN BARK, CAN'T I, EVEN IF I'M NOT ALLOWED TO TALK?
ALL RIGHT, YOU WIN, YOU PIGHEADED GREAT IDIOT! LET HIM OUT!
THERE'S MY SHIP, THE NASTIUPSET.

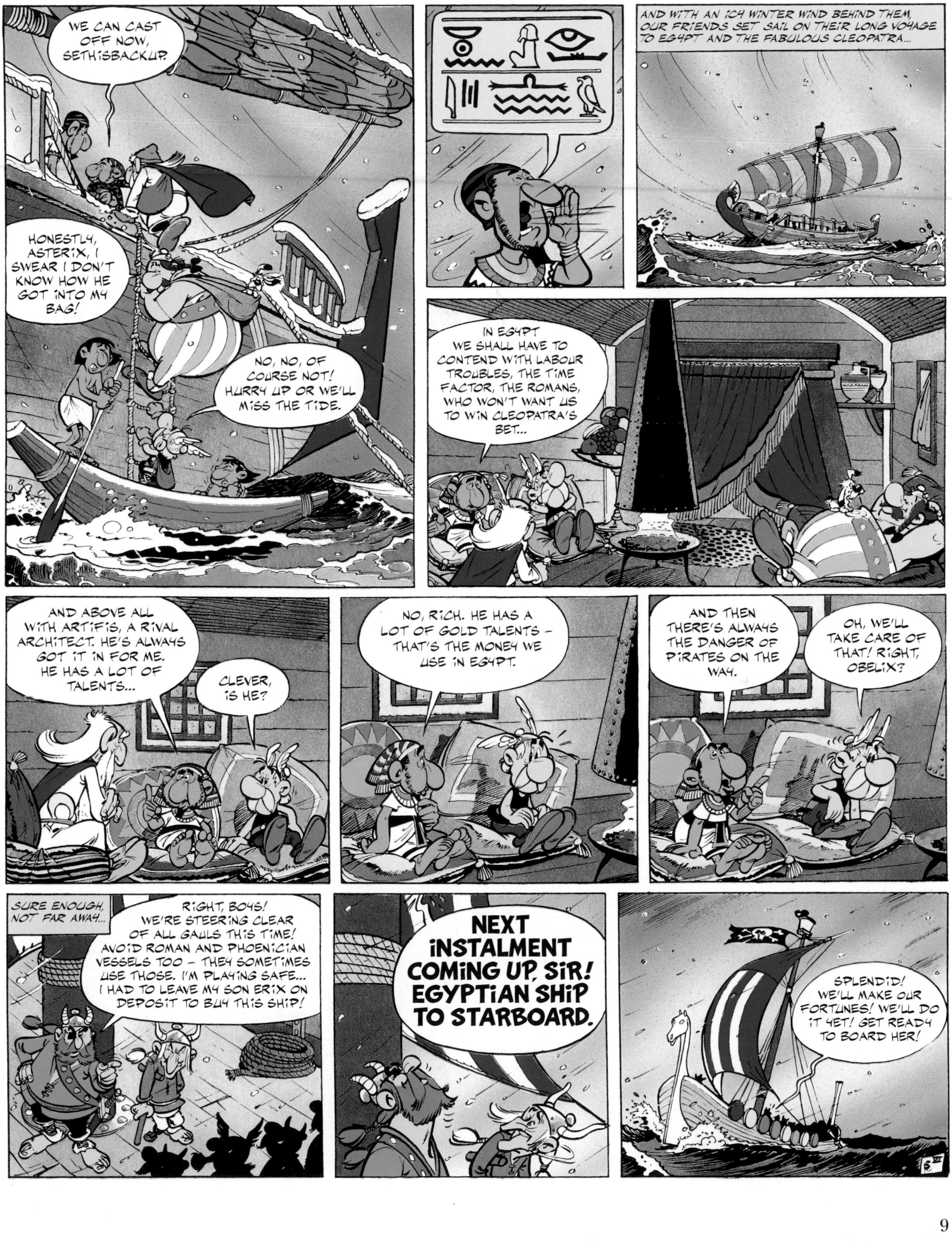
WE CAN CAST OFF NOW, SETHISBACKUP.
HONESTLY, ASTERIX, I SWEAR I DON'T KNOW HOW HE GOT INTO MY BAG!
NO, NO, OF COURSE NOT! HURRY UP OR WE'LL MISS THE TIDE.
AND WITH AN ICY WINTER WIND BEHIND THEM, OUR FRIENDS SET SAIL ON THEIR LONG VOYAGE TO EGYPT AND THE FABULOUS CLEOPATRA...
IN EGYPT WE SHALL HAVE TO CONTEND WITH LABOUR TROUBLES, THE TIME FACTOR, THE ROMANS, WHO WON'T WANT US TO WIN CLEOPATRA'S BET...
AND ABOVE ALL WITH ARTIFIS, A RIVAL ARCHITECT. HE'S ALWAYS GOT IT IN FOR ME. HE HAS A LOT OF TALENTS...
CLEVER, IS HE?
NO, RICH. HE HAS A LOT OF GOLD TALENTS – THAT'S THE MONEY WE USE IN EGYPT.
AND THEN THERE'S ALWAYS THE DANGER OF PIRATES ON THE WAY.
OH, WE'LL TAKE CARE OF THAT! RIGHT, OBELIX?
SURE ENOUGH, NOT FAR AWAY...
RIGHT, BOYS! WE'RE STEERING CLEAR OF ALL GAULS THIS TIME! AVOID ROMAN AND PHOENICIAN VESSELS TOO – THEY SOMETIMES USE THOSE. I'M PLAYING SAFE... I HAD TO LEAVE MY SON ERIX ON DEPOSIT TO BUY THIS SHIP!
NEXT INSTALMENT COMING UP, SIR! EGYPTIAN SHIP TO STARBOARD.
SPLENDID! WE'LL MAKE OUR FORTUNES! WE'LL DO IT YET! GET READY TO BOARD HER!

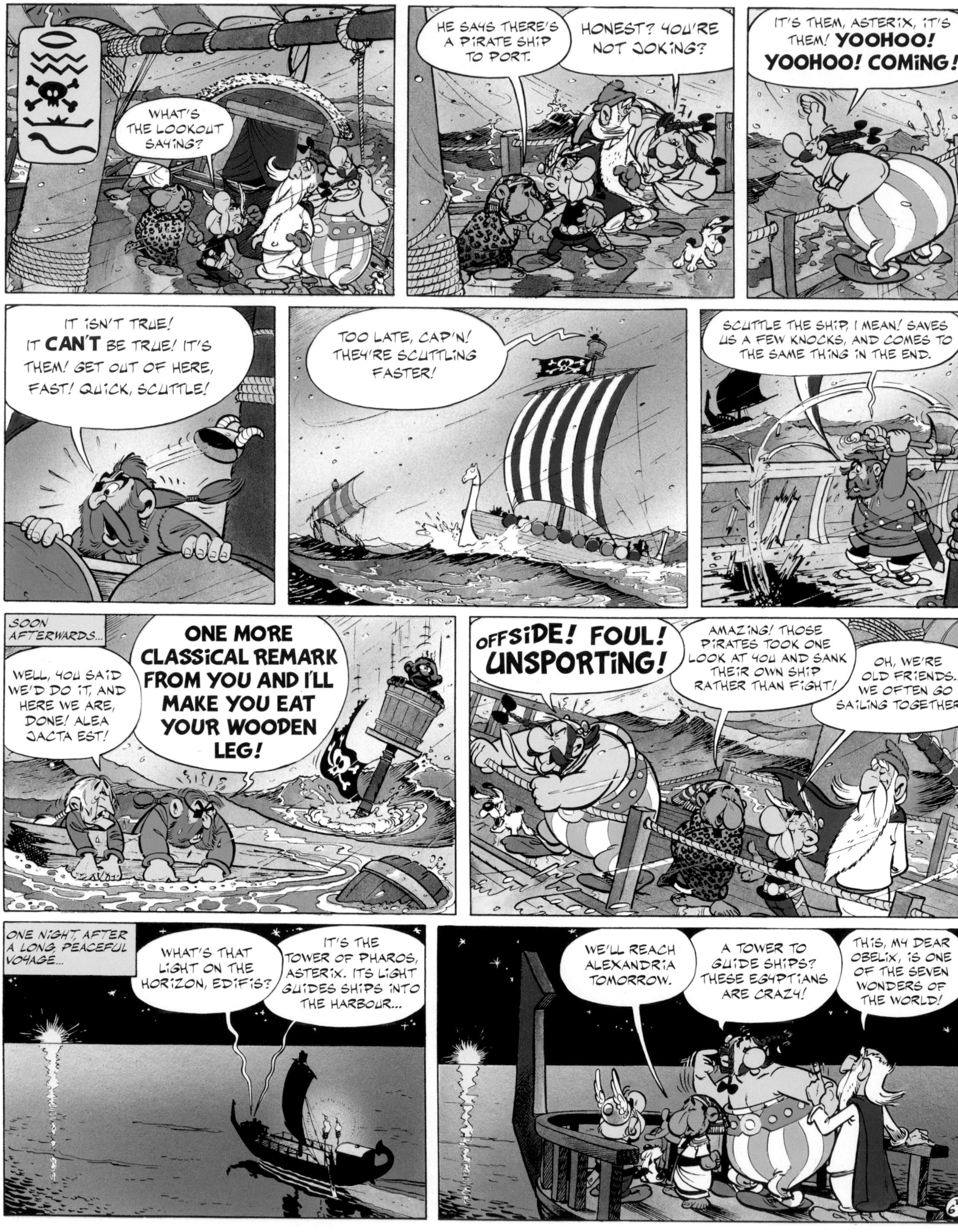
WHAT'S THE LOOKOUT SAYING?
HE SAYS THERE'S A PIRATE SHIP TO PORT.
HONEST? YOU'RE NOT JOKING?
IT'S THEM, ASTERIX, IT'S THEM! YOOHOO! YOOHOO! COMING!
IT ISN'T TRUE! IT CAN'T BE TRUE! IT'S THEM! GET OUT OF HERE, FAST! QUICK, SCUTTLE!
TOO LATE, CAP'N! THEY'RE SCUTTLING FASTER!
SCUTTLE THE SHIP, I MEAN! SAVES US A FEW KNOCKS, AND COMES TO THE SAME THING IN THE END.
SOON AFTERWARDS...
WELL, YOU SAID WE'D DO IT, AND HERE WE ARE, DONE! ALEA JACTA EST!
ONE MORE CLASSICAL REMARK FROM YOU AND I'LL MAKE YOU EAT YOUR WOODEN LEG!
OFFSIDE! FOUL! UNSPORTING!
AMAZING! THOSE PIRATES TOOK ONE LOOK AT YOU AND SANK THEIR OWN SHIP RATHER THAN FIGHT!
OH, WE'RE OLD FRIENDS... WE OFTEN GO SAILING TOGETHER.
ONE NIGHT, AFTER A LONG, PEACEFUL VOYAGE...
WHAT'S THAT LIGHT ON THE HORIZON, EDIFIS?
IT'S THE TOWER OF PHAROS, ASTERIX. ITS LIGHT GUIDES SHIPS INTO THE HARBOUR...
WE'LL REACH ALEXANDRIA TOMORROW.
A TOWER TO GUIDE SHIPS? THESE EGYPTIANS ARE CRAZY!
THIS, MY DEAR OBELIX, IS ONE OF THE SEVEN WONDERS OF THE WORLD!

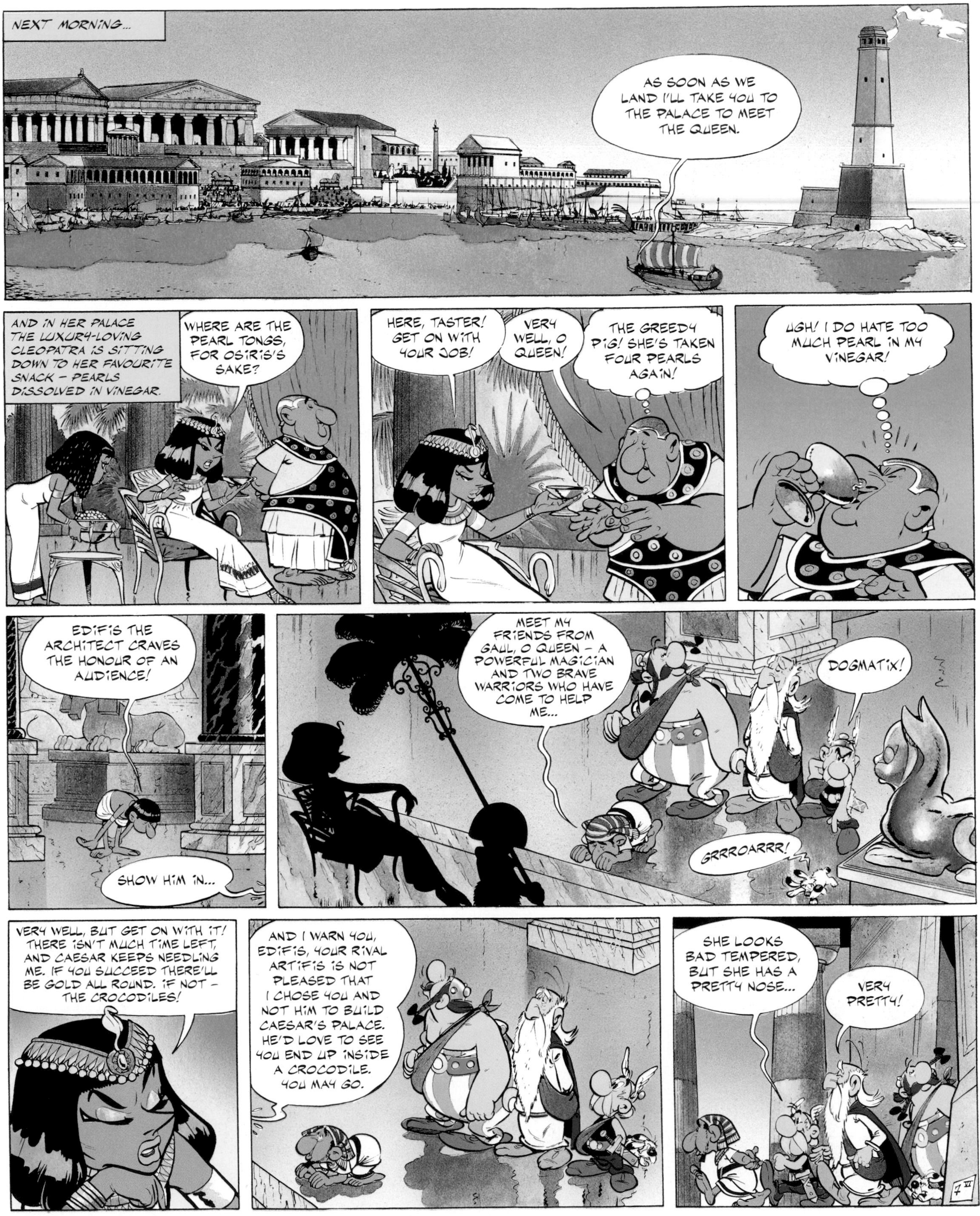
NEXT MORNING...
AS SOON AS WE LAND I'LL TAKE YOU TO THE PALACE TO MEET THE QUEEN.
AND IN HER PALACE THE LUXURY-LOVING CLEOPATRA IS SITTING DOWN TO HER FAVOURITE SNACK – PEARLS DISSOLVED IN VINEGAR.
WHERE ARE THE PEARL TONGS, FOR OSIRIS'S SAKE?
HERE, TASTER! GET ON WITH YOUR JOB!
VERY WELL, O QUEEN!
THE GREEDY PIG! SHE'S TAKEN FOUR PEARLS AGAIN!
UGH! I DO HATE TOO MUCH PEARL IN MY VINEGAR!
EDIFIS THE ARCHITECT CRAVES THE HONOUR OF AN AUDIENCE!
SHOW HIM IN...
MEET MY FRIENDS FROM GAUL, O QUEEN – A POWERFUL MAGICIAN AND TWO BRAVE WARRIORS WHO HAVE COME TO HELP ME...
DOGMATIX!
GRRROARRR!
VERY WELL, BUT GET ON WITH IT! THERE ISN'T MUCH TIME LEFT, AND CAESAR KEEPS NEEDLING ME. IF YOU SUCCEED THERE'LL BE GOLD ALL ROUND. IF NOT – THE CROCODILES!
AND I WARN YOU, EDIFIS, YOUR RIVAL ARTIFIS IS NOT PLEASED THAT I CHOSE YOU AND NOT HIM TO BUILD CAESAR'S PALACE. HE'D LOVE TO SEE YOU END UP INSIDE A CROCODILE. YOU MAY GO.
SHE LOOKS BAD TEMPERED, BUT SHE HAS A PRETTY NOSE...
VERY PRETTY!

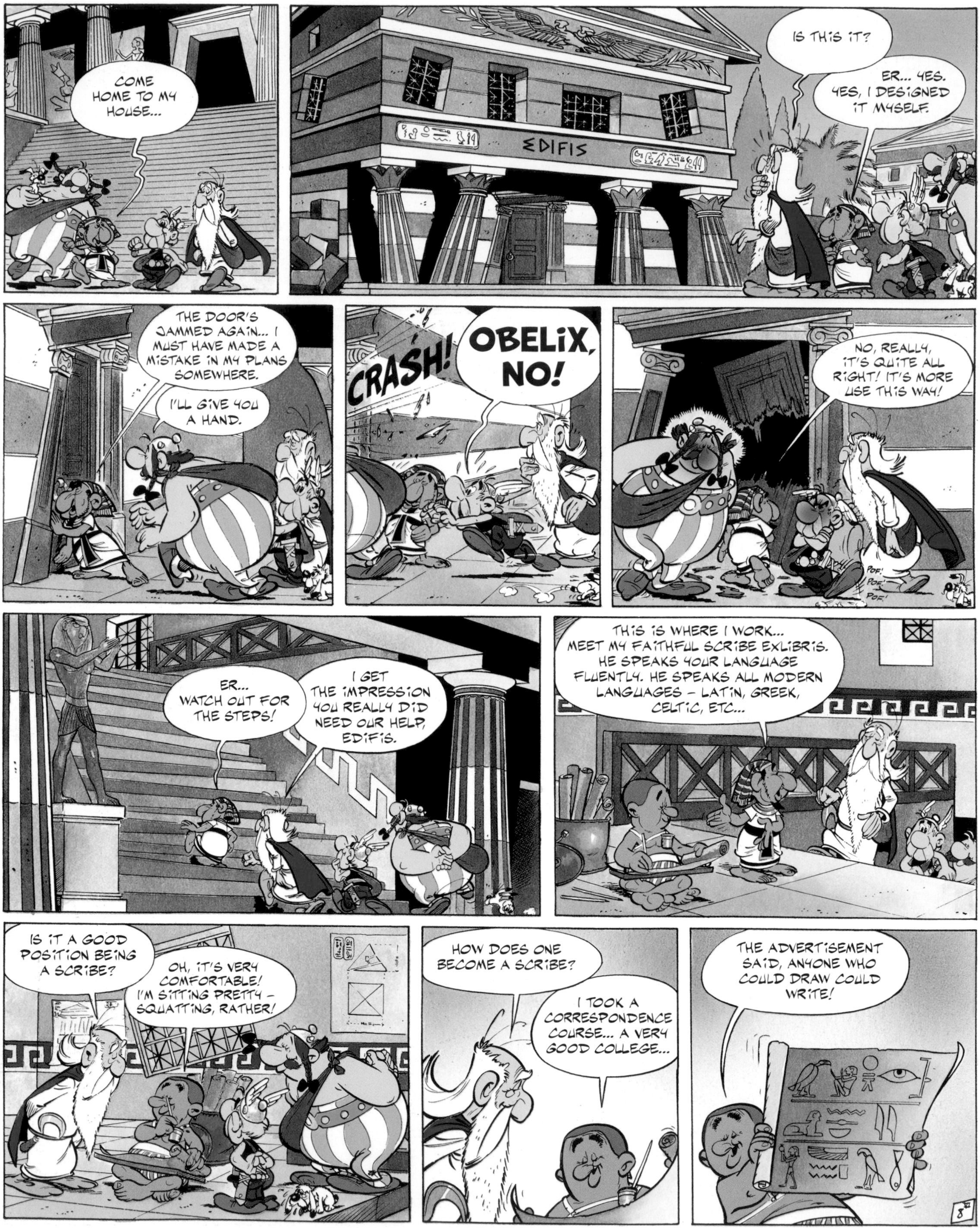
COME HOME TO MY HOUSE...
EDIFIS
IS THIS IT?
ER... YES. YES, I DESIGNED IT MYSELF.
THE DOOR'S JAMMED AGAIN... I MUST HAVE MADE A MISTAKE IN MY PLANS SOMEWHERE.
I'LL GIVE YOU A HAND.
CRASH!
OBELIX, NO!
NO, REALLY, IT'S QUITE ALL RIGHT! IT'S MORE USE THIS WAY!
POF! POF! POF!
ER... WATCH OUT FOR THE STEPS!
I GET THE IMPRESSION YOU REALLY DID NEED OUR HELP, EDIFIS.
THIS IS WHERE I WORK... MEET MY FAITHFUL SCRIBE EXLIBRIS. HE SPEAKS YOUR LANGUAGE FLUENTLY. HE SPEAKS ALL MODERN LANGUAGES – LATIN, GREEK, CELTIC, ETC...
IS IT A GOOD POSITION BEING A SCRIBE?
OH, IT'S VERY COMFORTABLE! I'M SITTING PRETTY – SQUATTING, RATHER!
HOW DOES ONE BECOME A SCRIBE?
I TOOK A CORRESPONDENCE COURSE... A VERY GOOD COLLEGE...
THE ADVERTISEMENT SAID, ANYONE WHO COULD DRAW COULD WRITE!

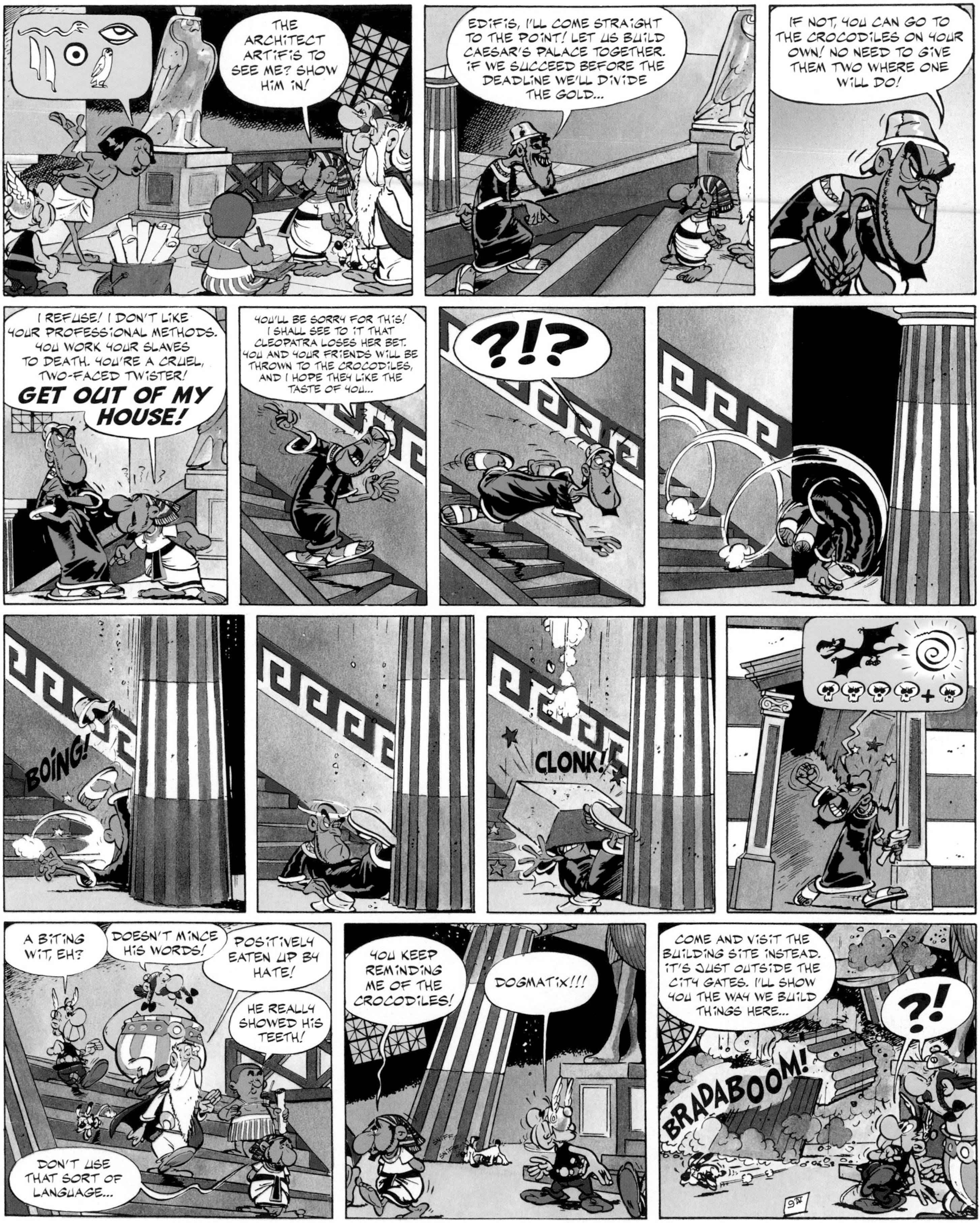
THE ARCHITECT ARTIFIS TO SEE ME? SHOW HIM IN!
EDIFIS, I'LL COME STRAIGHT TO THE POINT! LET US BUILD CAESAR'S PALACE TOGETHER. IF WE SUCCEED BEFORE THE DEADLINE WE'LL DIVIDE THE GOLD...
IF NOT, YOU CAN GO TO THE CROCODILES ON YOUR OWN! NO NEED TO GIVE THEM TWO WHERE ONE WILL DO!
I REFUSE! I DON'T LIKE YOUR PROFESSIONAL METHODS. YOU WORK YOUR SLAVES TO DEATH. YOU'RE A CRUEL, TWO-FACED TWISTER!
GET OUT OF MY HOUSE!
YOU'LL BE SORRY FOR THIS! I SHALL SEE TO IT THAT CLEOPATRA LOSES HER BET. YOU AND YOUR FRIENDS WILL BE THROWN TO THE CROCODILES, AND I HOPE THEY LIKE THE TASTE OF YOU...
?!?
BOING!
CLONK!
A BITING WIT, EH?
DOESN'T MINCE HIS WORDS!
POSITIVELY EATEN UP BY HATE!
HE REALLY SHOWED HIS TEETH!
DON'T USE THAT SORT OF LANGUAGE...
YOU KEEP REMINDING ME OF THE CROCODILES!
DOGMATIX!!!
COME AND VISIT THE BUILDING SITE INSTEAD. IT'S JUST OUTSIDE THE CITY GATES. I'LL SHOW YOU THE WAY WE BUILD THINGS HERE...
?!
BRADABOOM!

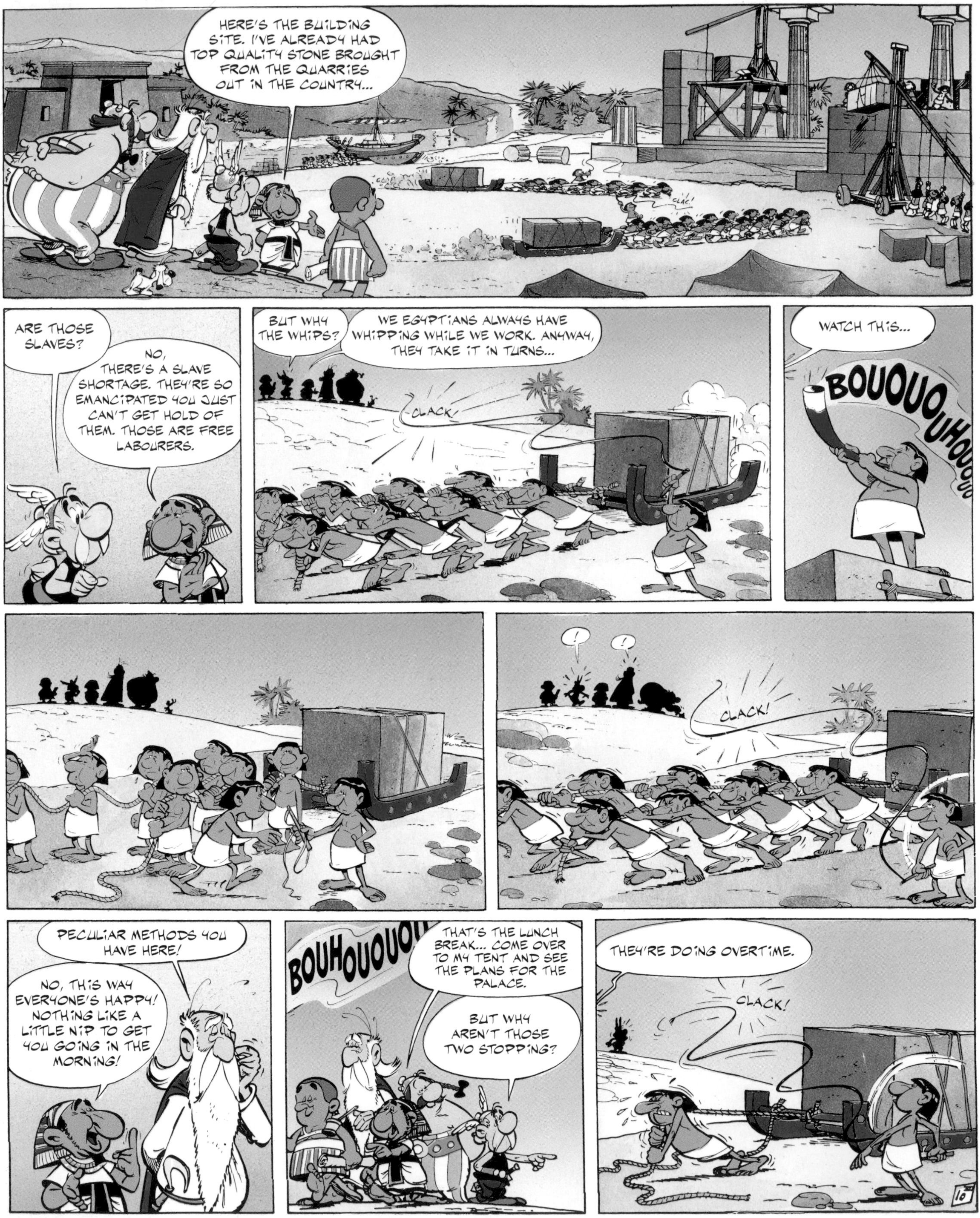
HERE'S THE BUILDING SITE. I'VE ALREADY HAD TOP QUALITY STONE BROUGHT FROM THE QUARRIES OUT IN THE COUNTRY...
CLAC!
ARE THOSE SLAVES?
NO, THERE'S A SLAVE SHORTAGE. THEY'RE SO EMANCIPATED YOU JUST CAN'T GET HOLD OF THEM. THOSE ARE FREE LABOURERS.
BUT WHY THE WHIPS?
WE EGYPTIANS ALWAYS HAVE WHIPPING WHILE WE WORK. ANYWAY, THEY TAKE IT IN TURNS...
CLACK!
WATCH THIS...
BOUOUOUHOUOUO
!
!
CLACK!
PECULIAR METHODS YOU HAVE HERE!
NO, THIS WAY EVERYONE'S HAPPY! NOTHING LIKE A LITTLE NIP TO GET YOU GOING IN THE MORNING!
BOUHOUOUOU
THAT'S THE LUNCH BREAK... COME OVER TO MY TENT AND SEE THE PLANS FOR THE PALACE.
BUT WHY AREN'T THOSE TWO STOPPING?
THEY'RE DOING OVERTIME.
CLACK!

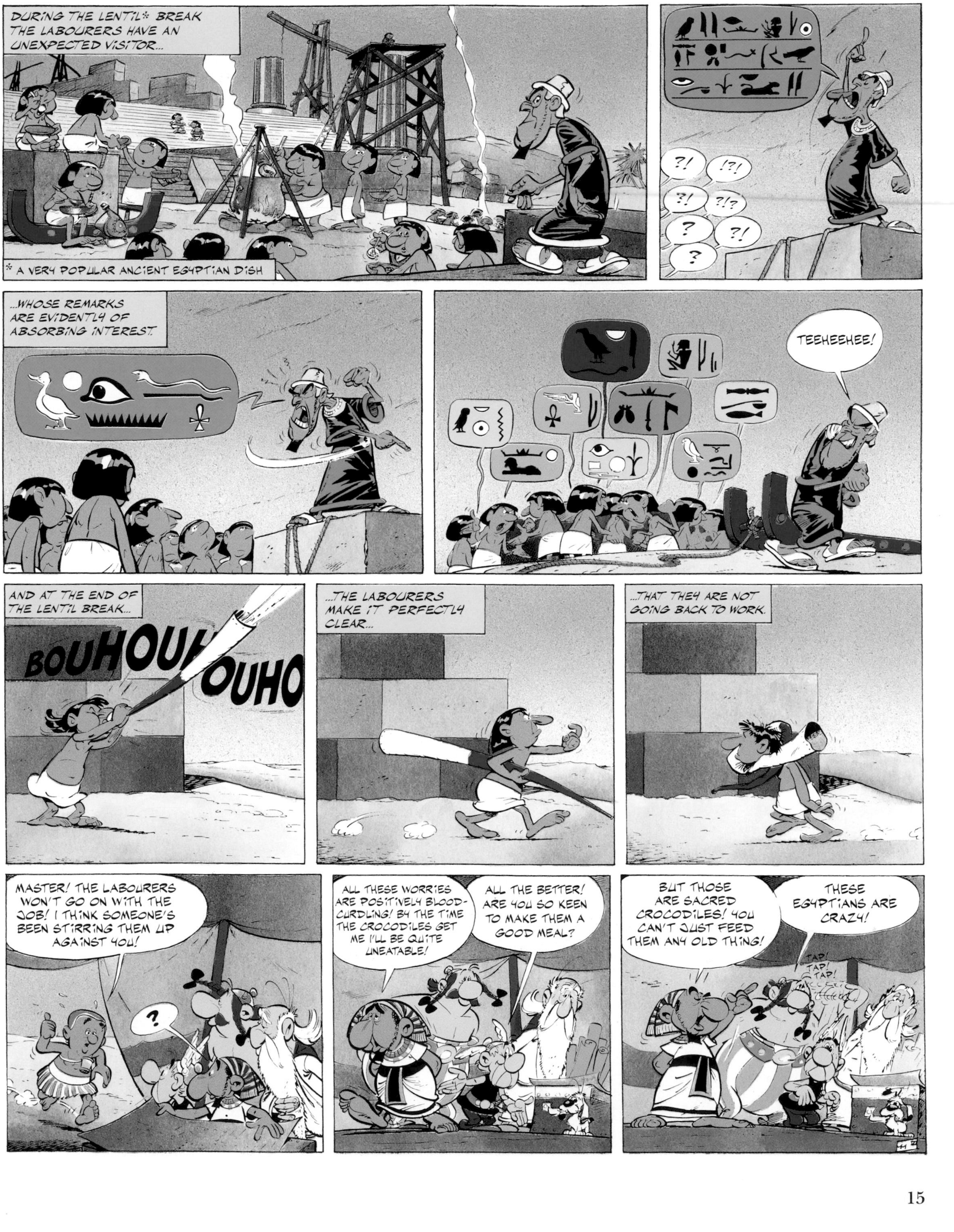
DURING THE LENTIL* BREAK THE LABOURERS HAVE AN UNEXPECTED VISITOR...
* A VERY POPULAR ANCIENT EGYPTIAN DISH
?! !?! ?! ?!? ? ?! ?
...WHOSE REMARKS ARE EVIDENTLY OF ABSORBING INTEREST.
TEEHEEHEE!
AND AT THE END OF THE LENTIL BREAK...
BOUHOUHOUHO
...THE LABOURERS MAKE IT PERFECTLY CLEAR...
...THAT THEY ARE NOT GOING BACK TO WORK.
MASTER! THE LABOURERS WON'T GO ON WITH THE JOB! I THINK SOMEONE'S BEEN STIRRING THEM UP AGAINST YOU!
?
ALL THESE WORRIES ARE POSITIVELY BLOOD-CURDLING! BY THE TIME THE CROCODILES GET ME I'LL BE QUITE UNEATABLE!
ALL THE BETTER! ARE YOU SO KEEN TO MAKE THEM A GOOD MEAL?
BUT THOSE ARE SACRED CROCODILES! YOU CAN'T JUST FEED THEM ANY OLD THING!
THESE EGYPTIANS ARE CRAZY!
TAP! TAP! TAP!

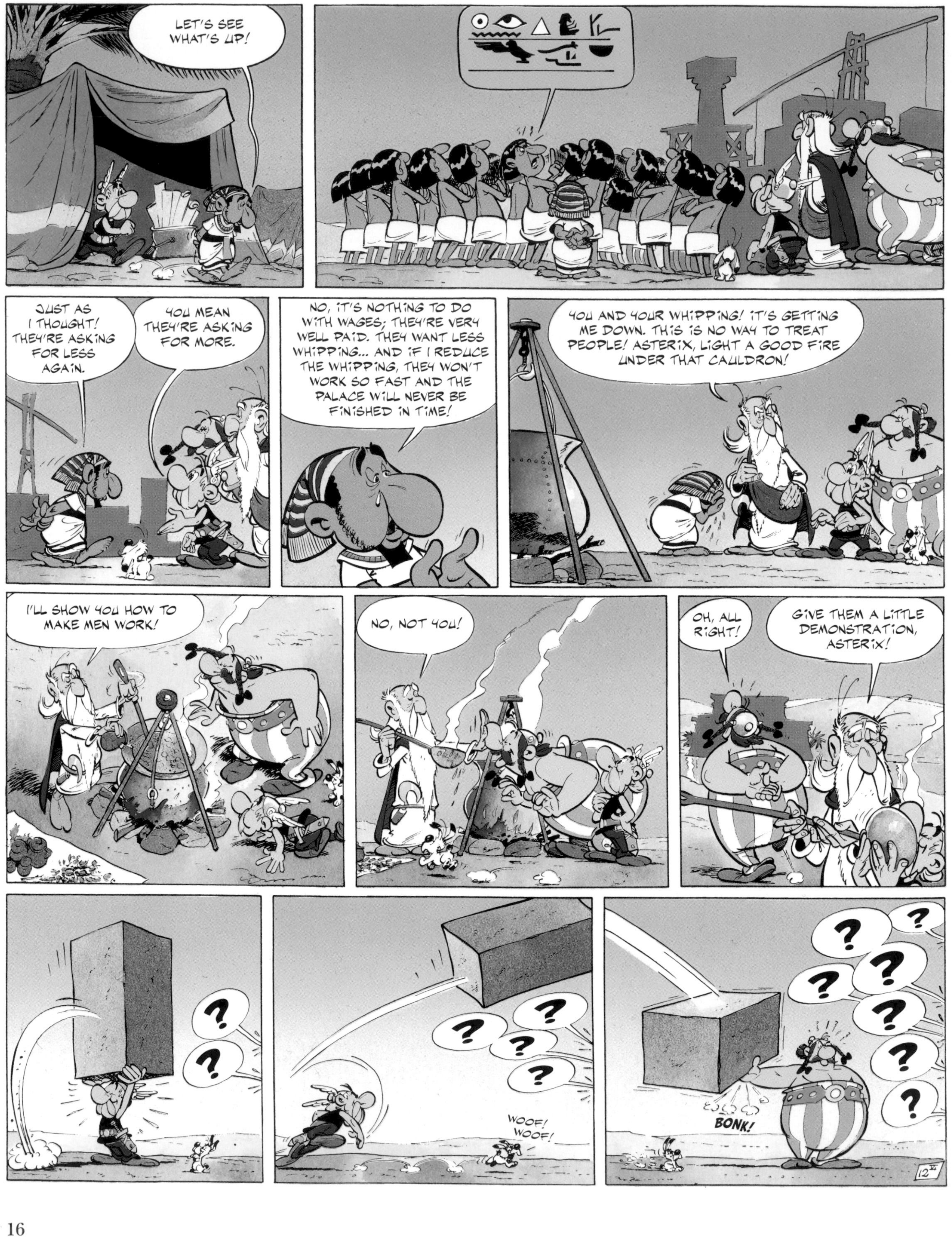
LET'S SEE WHAT'S UP!
JUST AS I THOUGHT! THEY'RE ASKING FOR LESS AGAIN.
YOU MEAN THEY'RE ASKING FOR MORE.
NO, IT'S NOTHING TO DO WITH WAGES; THEY'RE VERY WELL PAID. THEY WANT LESS WHIPPING... AND IF I REDUCE THE WHIPPING, THEY WON'T WORK SO FAST AND THE PALACE WILL NEVER BE FINISHED IN TIME!
YOU AND YOUR WHIPPING! IT'S GETTING ME DOWN. THIS IS NO WAY TO TREAT PEOPLE! ASTERIX, LIGHT A GOOD FIRE UNDER THAT CAULDRON!
I'LL SHOW YOU HOW TO MAKE MEN WORK!
NO, NOT YOU!
OH, ALL RIGHT!
GIVE THEM A LITTLE DEMONSTRATION, ASTERIX!
WOOF! WOOF!
BONK!

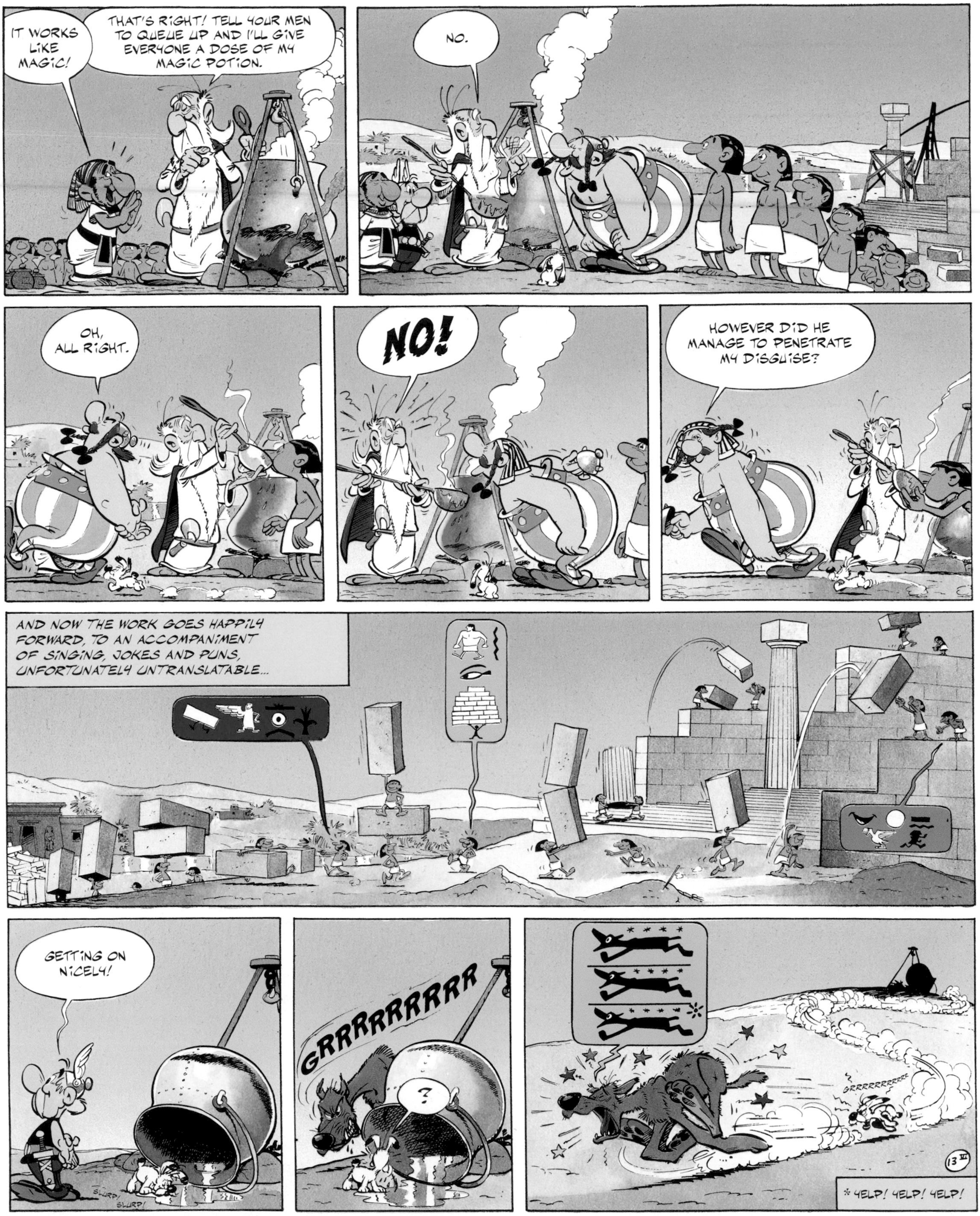

IT WORKS LIKE MAGIC!
THAT'S RIGHT! TELL YOUR MEN TO QUEUE UP AND I'LL GIVE EVERYONE A DOSE OF MY MAGIC POTION.
NO.
OH, ALL RIGHT.
NO!
HOWEVER DID HE MANAGE TO PENETRATE MY DISGUISE?
AND NOW THE WORK GOES HAPPILY FORWARD, TO AN ACCOMPANIMENT OF SINGING, JOKES AND PUNS, UNFORTUNATELY UNTRANSLATABLE...
GETTING ON NICELY!
SLURP! SLURP!
GRRRRRRRRRR
?
GRRRRRRRRR
* YELP! YELP! YELP!

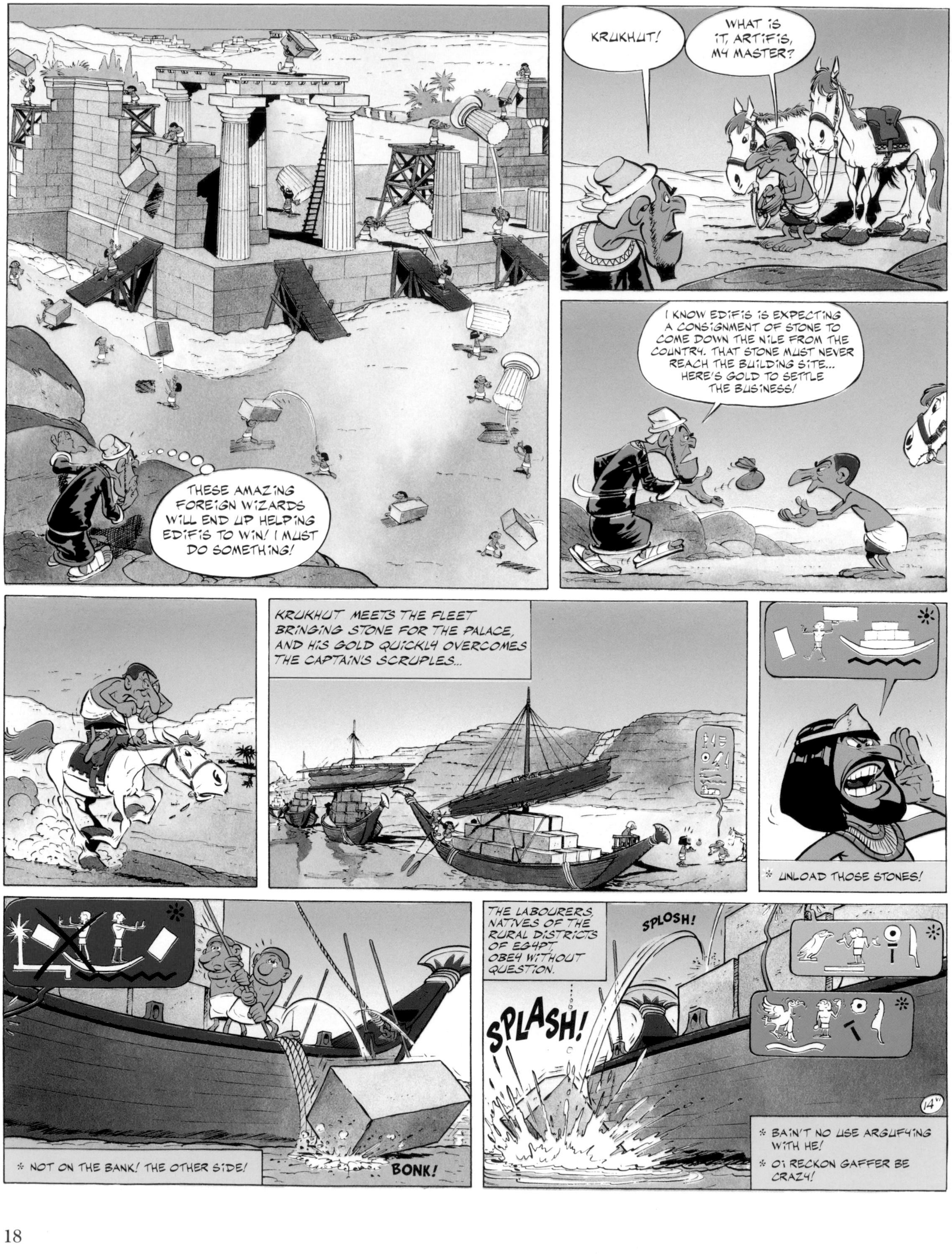
THESE AMAZING FOREIGN WIZARDS WILL END UP HELPING EDIFIS TO WIN! I MUST DO SOMETHING!
KRUKHUT!
WHAT IS IT, ARTIFIS, MY MASTER?
I KNOW EDIFIS IS EXPECTING A CONSIGNMENT OF STONE TO COME DOWN THE NILE FROM THE COUNTRY. THAT STONE MUST NEVER REACH THE BUILDING SITE... HERE'S GOLD TO SETTLE THE BUSINESS!
KRUKHUT MEETS THE FLEET BRINGING STONE FOR THE PALACE, AND HIS GOLD QUICKLY OVERCOMES THE CAPTAIN'S SCRUPLES...
* UNLOAD THOSE STONES!
* NOT ON THE BANK! THE OTHER SIDE!
BONK!
THE LABOURERS, NATIVES OF THE RURAL DISTRICTS OF EGYPT, OBEY WITHOUT QUESTION.
SPLOSH!
SPLASH!
* BAIN'T NO USE ARGUFYING WITH HE!
* OI RECKON GAFFER BE CRAZY!

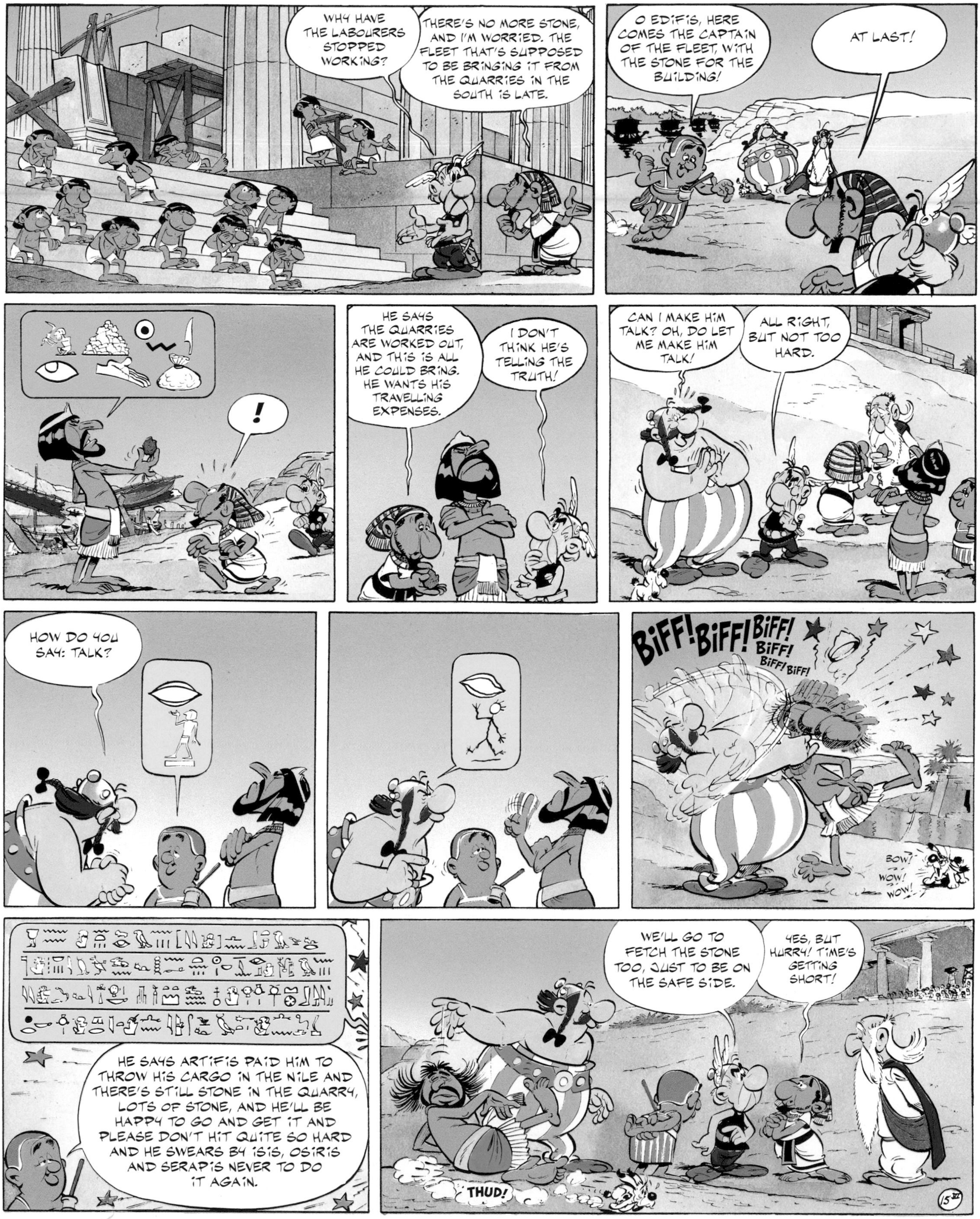
WHY HAVE THE LABOURERS STOPPED WORKING?
THERE'S NO MORE STONE, AND I'M WORRIED. THE FLEET THAT'S SUPPOSED TO BE BRINGING IT FROM THE QUARRIES IN THE SOUTH IS LATE.
O EDIFIS, HERE COMES THE CAPTAIN OF THE FLEET, WITH THE STONE FOR THE BUILDING!
AT LAST!
!
HE SAYS THE QUARRIES ARE WORKED OUT, AND THIS IS ALL HE COULD BRING. HE WANTS HIS TRAVELLING EXPENSES.
I DON'T THINK HE'S TELLING THE TRUTH!
CAN I MAKE HIM TALK? OH, DO LET ME MAKE HIM TALK!
ALL RIGHT, BUT NOT TOO HARD.
HOW DO YOU SAY: TALK?
BIFF! BIFF! BIFF! BIFF! BIFF! BIFF!
BOW! WOW! WOW!
HE SAYS ARTIFIS PAID HIM TO THROW HIS CARGO IN THE NILE AND THERE'S STILL STONE IN THE QUARRY, LOTS OF STONE, AND HE'LL BE HAPPY TO GO AND GET IT AND PLEASE DON'T HIT QUITE SO HARD AND HE SWEARS BY ISIS, OSIRIS AND SERAPIS NEVER TO DO IT AGAIN.
WE'LL GO TO FETCH THE STONE TOO, JUST TO BE ON THE SAFE SIDE.
YES, BUT HURRY! TIME'S GETTING SHORT!
THUD!

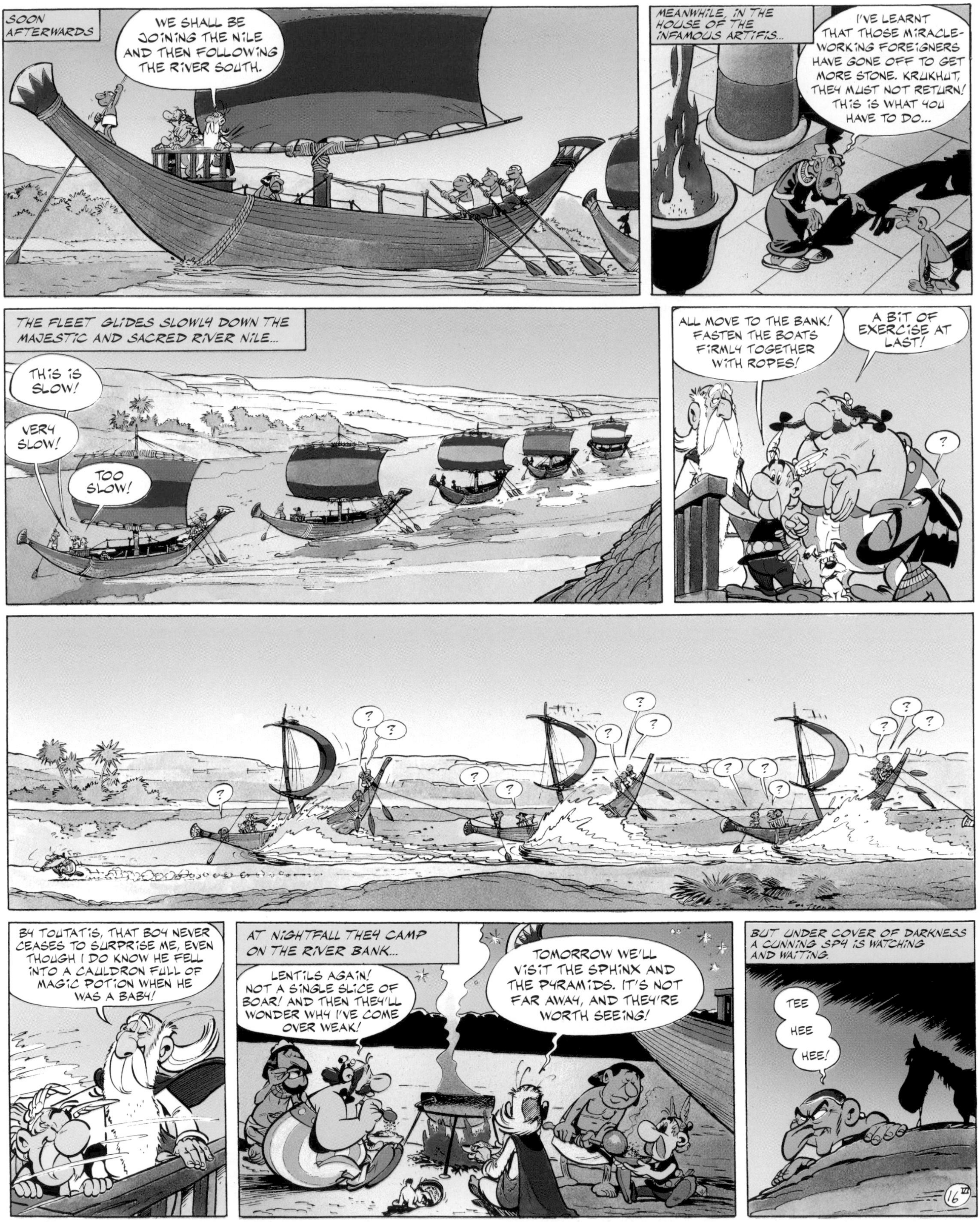

SOON AFTERWARDS
WE SHALL BE JOINING THE NILE AND THEN FOLLOWING THE RIVER SOUTH.
MEANWHILE, IN THE HOUSE OF THE INFAMOUS ARTIFIS...
I'VE LEARNT THAT THOSE MIRACLE-WORKING FOREIGNERS HAVE GONE OFF TO GET MORE STONE. KRUKHUT, THEY MUST NOT RETURN! THIS IS WHAT YOU HAVE TO DO...
THE FLEET GLIDES SLOWLY DOWN THE MAJESTIC AND SACRED RIVER NILE...
THIS IS SLOW!
VERY SLOW!
TOO SLOW!
ALL MOVE TO THE BANK! FASTEN THE BOATS FIRMLY TOGETHER WITH ROPES!
A BIT OF EXERCISE AT LAST!
?
BY TOUTATIS, THAT BOY NEVER CEASES TO SURPRISE ME, EVEN THOUGH I DO KNOW HE FELL INTO A CAULDRON FULL OF MAGIC POTION WHEN HE WAS A BABY!
AT NIGHTFALL THEY CAMP ON THE RIVER BANK...
LENTILS AGAIN! NOT A SINGLE SLICE OF BOAR! AND THEN THEY'LL WONDER WHY I'VE COME OVER WEAK!
TOMORROW WE'LL VISIT THE SPHINX AND THE PYRAMIDS. IT'S NOT FAR AWAY, AND THEY'RE WORTH SEEING!
BUT UNDER COVER OF DARKNESS A CUNNING SPY IS WATCHING AND WAITING.
TEE
HEE
HEE!

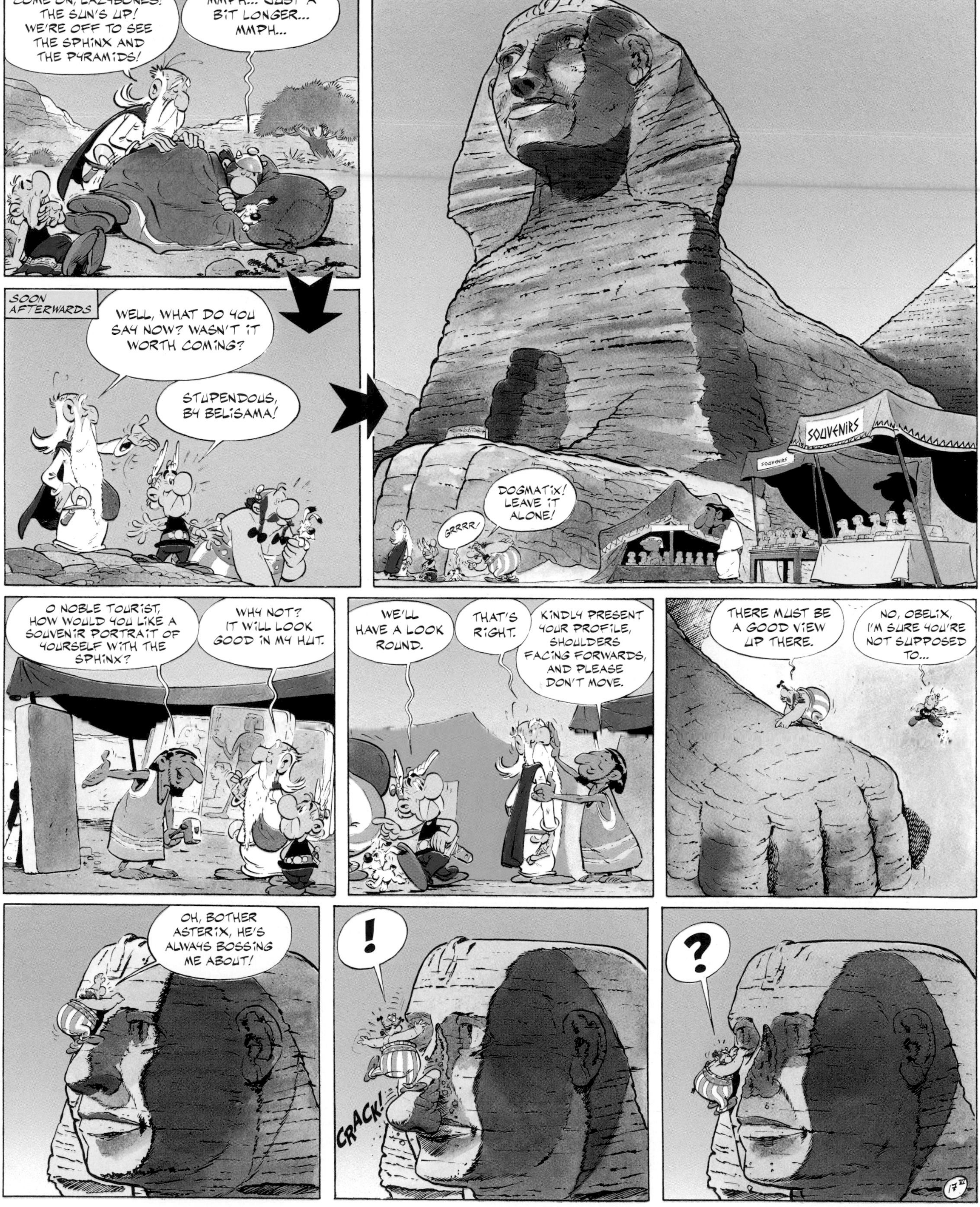

COME ON, LAZYBONES! THE SUN'S UP! WE'RE OFF TO SEE THE SPHINX AND THE PYRAMIDS!
MMPH... JUST A BIT LONGER... MMPH...
SOON AFTERWARDS
WELL, WHAT DO YOU SAY NOW? WASN'T IT WORTH COMING?
STUPENDOUS, BY BELISAMA!
SOUVENIRS
SOUVENIRS
GRRRR!
DOGMATIX! LEAVE IT ALONE!
O NOBLE TOURIST, HOW WOULD YOU LIKE A SOUVENIR PORTRAIT OF YOURSELF WITH THE SPHINX?
WHY NOT? IT WILL LOOK GOOD IN MY HUT.
WE'LL HAVE A LOOK ROUND.
THAT'S RIGHT.
KINDLY PRESENT YOUR PROFILE, SHOULDERS FACING FORWARDS, AND PLEASE DON'T MOVE.
THERE MUST BE A GOOD VIEW UP THERE.
NO, OBELIX, I'M SURE YOU'RE NOT SUPPOSED TO...
OH, BOTHER ASTERIX, HE'S ALWAYS BOSSING ME ABOUT!
!
CRACK!
?

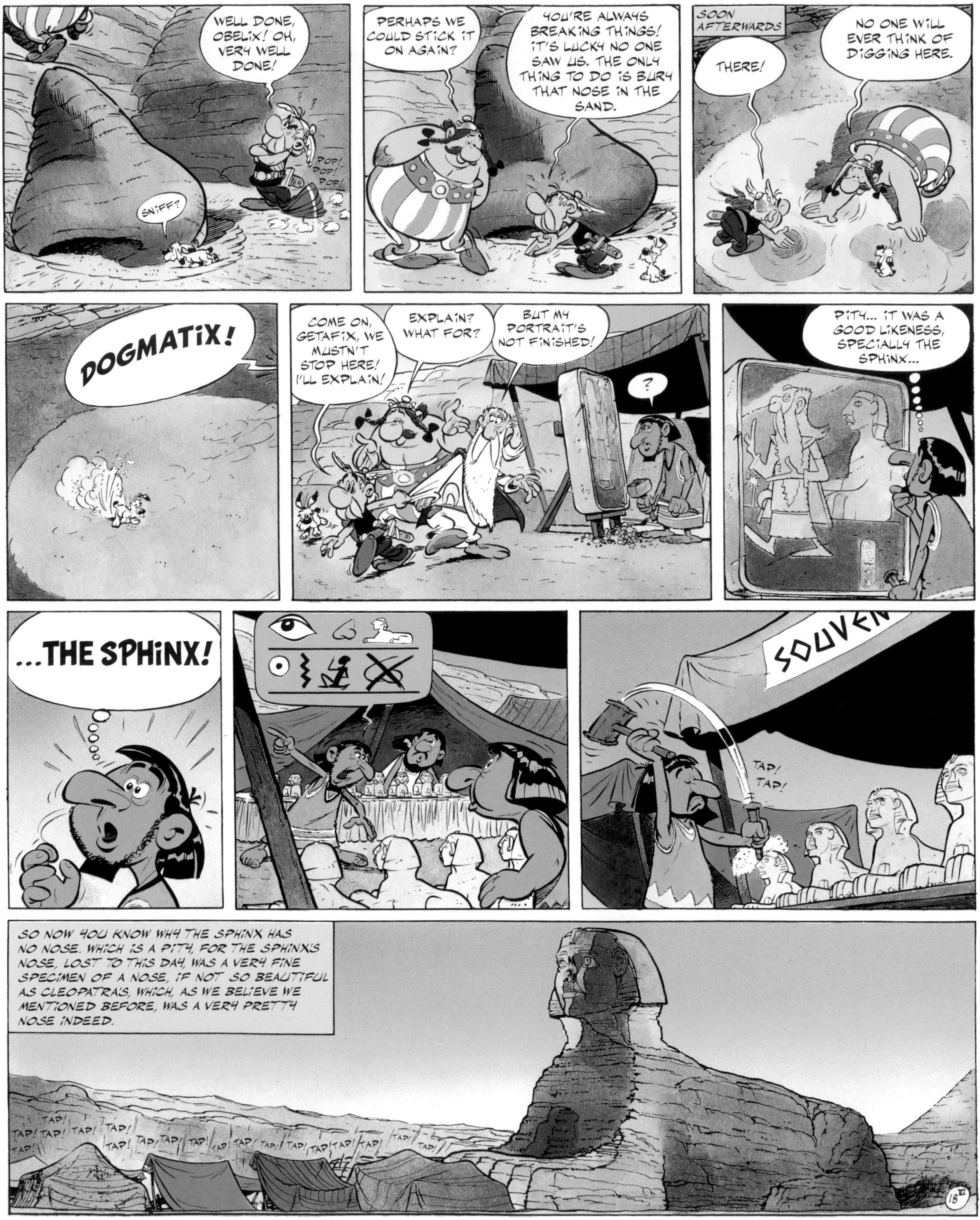
WELL DONE, OBELIX! OH, VERY WELL DONE!
POF! POF! POF!
SNIFF?
PERHAPS WE COULD STICK IT ON AGAIN?
YOU'RE ALWAYS BREAKING THINGS! IT'S LUCKY NO ONE SAW US. THE ONLY THING TO DO IS BURY THAT NOSE IN THE SAND.
SOON AFTERWARDS
THERE!
NO ONE WILL EVER THINK OF DIGGING HERE.
DOGMATIX!
COME ON, GETAFIX, WE MUSTN'T STOP HERE! I'LL EXPLAIN!
EXPLAIN? WHAT FOR?
BUT MY PORTRAIT'S NOT FINISHED!
?
PITY... IT WAS A GOOD LIKENESS, SPECIALLY THE SPHINX...
...THE SPHINX!
SOUVEN
TAP! TAP!
SO NOW YOU KNOW WHY THE SPHINX HAS NO NOSE. WHICH IS A PITY, FOR THE SPHINX'S NOSE, LOST TO THIS DAY, WAS A VERY FINE SPECIMEN OF A NOSE, IF NOT SO BEAUTIFUL AS CLEOPATRA'S, WHICH, AS WE BELIEVE WE MENTIONED BEFORE, WAS A VERY PRETTY NOSE INDEED.
TAP! TAP! TAP! TAP! TAP! TAP! TAP! TAP! TAP! TAP! TAP! TAP! TAP! TAP! TAP! TAP! TAP!

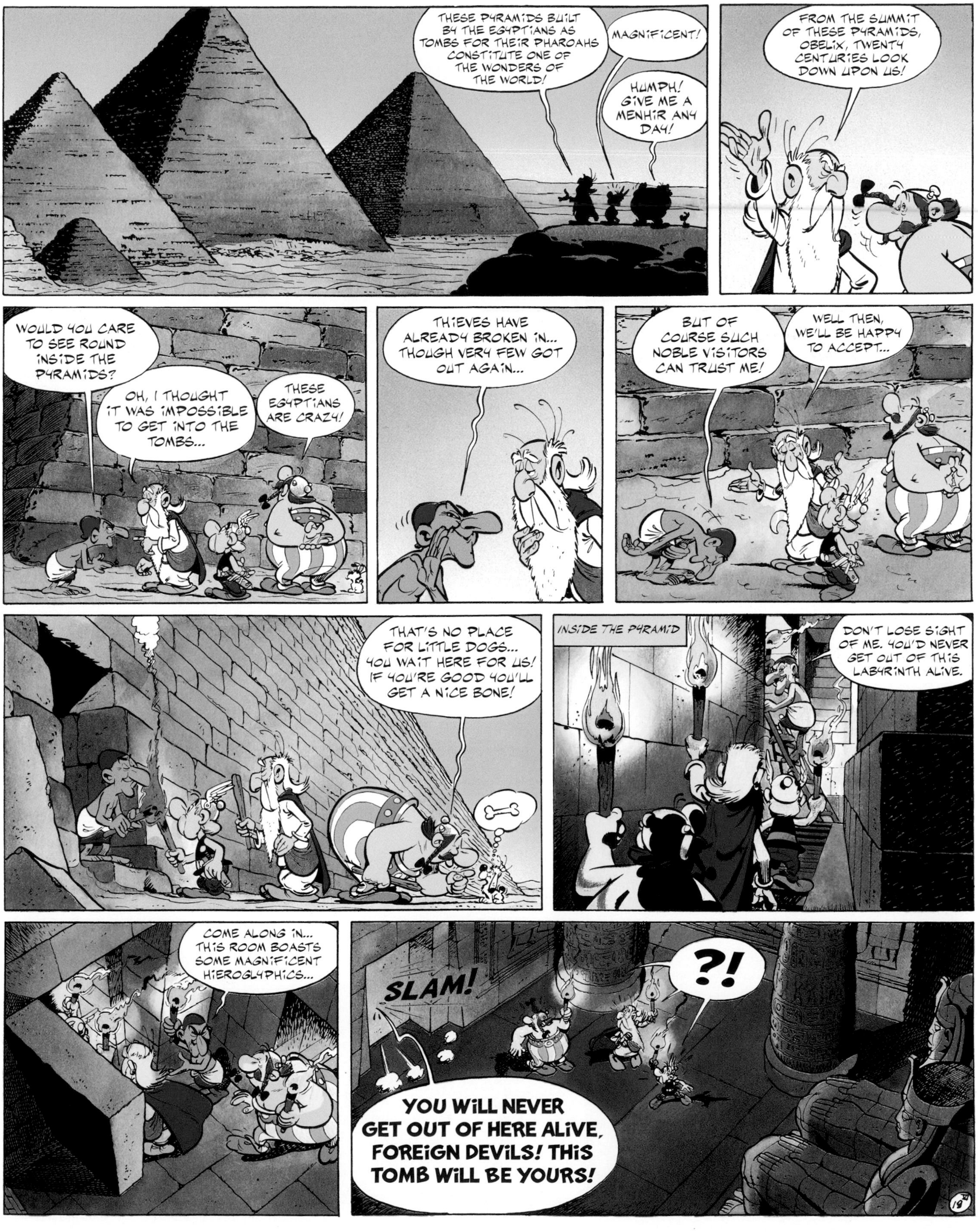

THESE PYRAMIDS BUILT BY THE EGYPTIANS AS TOMBS FOR THEIR PHAROAHS CONSTITUTE ONE OF THE WONDERS OF THE WORLD!
MAGNIFICENT!
HUMPH! GIVE ME A MENHIR ANY DAY!
FROM THE SUMMIT OF THESE PYRAMIDS, OBELIX, TWENTY CENTURIES LOOK DOWN UPON US!
WOULD YOU CARE TO SEE ROUND INSIDE THE PYRAMIDS?
OH, I THOUGHT IT WAS IMPOSSIBLE TO GET INTO THE TOMBS...
THESE EGYPTIANS ARE CRAZY!
THIEVES HAVE ALREADY BROKEN IN... THOUGH VERY FEW GOT OUT AGAIN...
BUT OF COURSE SUCH NOBLE VISITORS CAN TRUST ME!
WELL THEN, WE'LL BE HAPPY TO ACCEPT...
THAT'S NO PLACE FOR LITTLE DOGS... YOU WAIT HERE FOR US! IF YOU'RE GOOD YOU'LL GET A NICE BONE!
INSIDE THE PYRAMID
DON'T LOSE SIGHT OF ME. YOU'D NEVER GET OUT OF THIS LABYRINTH ALIVE.
COME ALONG IN... THIS ROOM BOASTS SOME MAGNIFICENT HIEROGLYPHICS...
SLAM!
?!
YOU WILL NEVER GET OUT OF HERE ALIVE, FOREIGN DEVILS! THIS TOMB WILL BE YOURS!

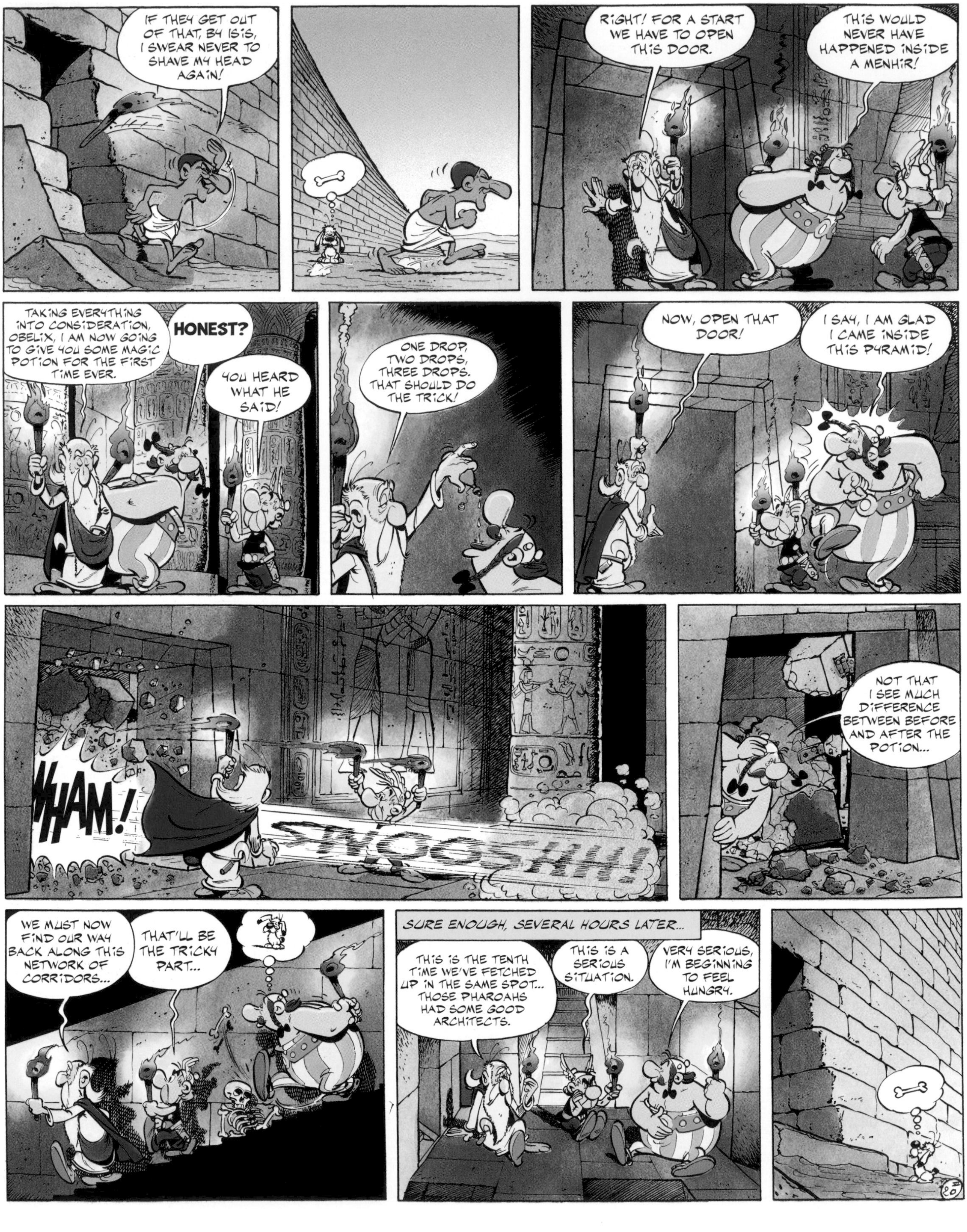

IF THEY GET OUT OF THAT, BY ISIS, I SWEAR NEVER TO SHAVE MY HEAD AGAIN!
RIGHT! FOR A START WE HAVE TO OPEN THIS DOOR.
THIS WOULD NEVER HAVE HAPPENED INSIDE A MENHIR!
TAKING EVERYTHING INTO CONSIDERATION, OBELIX, I AM NOW GOING TO GIVE YOU SOME MAGIC POTION FOR THE FIRST TIME EVER.
HONEST?
YOU HEARD WHAT HE SAID!
ONE DROP, TWO DROPS, THREE DROPS. THAT SHOULD DO THE TRICK!
NOW, OPEN THAT DOOR!
I SAY, I AM GLAD I CAME INSIDE THIS PYRAMID!
WHAM!
SWOOSHH!
NOT THAT I SEE MUCH DIFFERENCE BETWEEN BEFORE AND AFTER THE POTION...
WE MUST NOW FIND OUR WAY BACK ALONG THIS NETWORK OF CORRIDORS...
THAT'LL BE THE TRICKY PART...
SURE ENOUGH, SEVERAL HOURS LATER...
THIS IS THE TENTH TIME WE'VE FETCHED UP IN THE SAME SPOT... THOSE PHAROAHS HAD SOME GOOD ARCHITECTS.
THIS IS A SERIOUS SITUATION.
VERY SERIOUS, I'M BEGINNING TO FEEL HUNGRY.

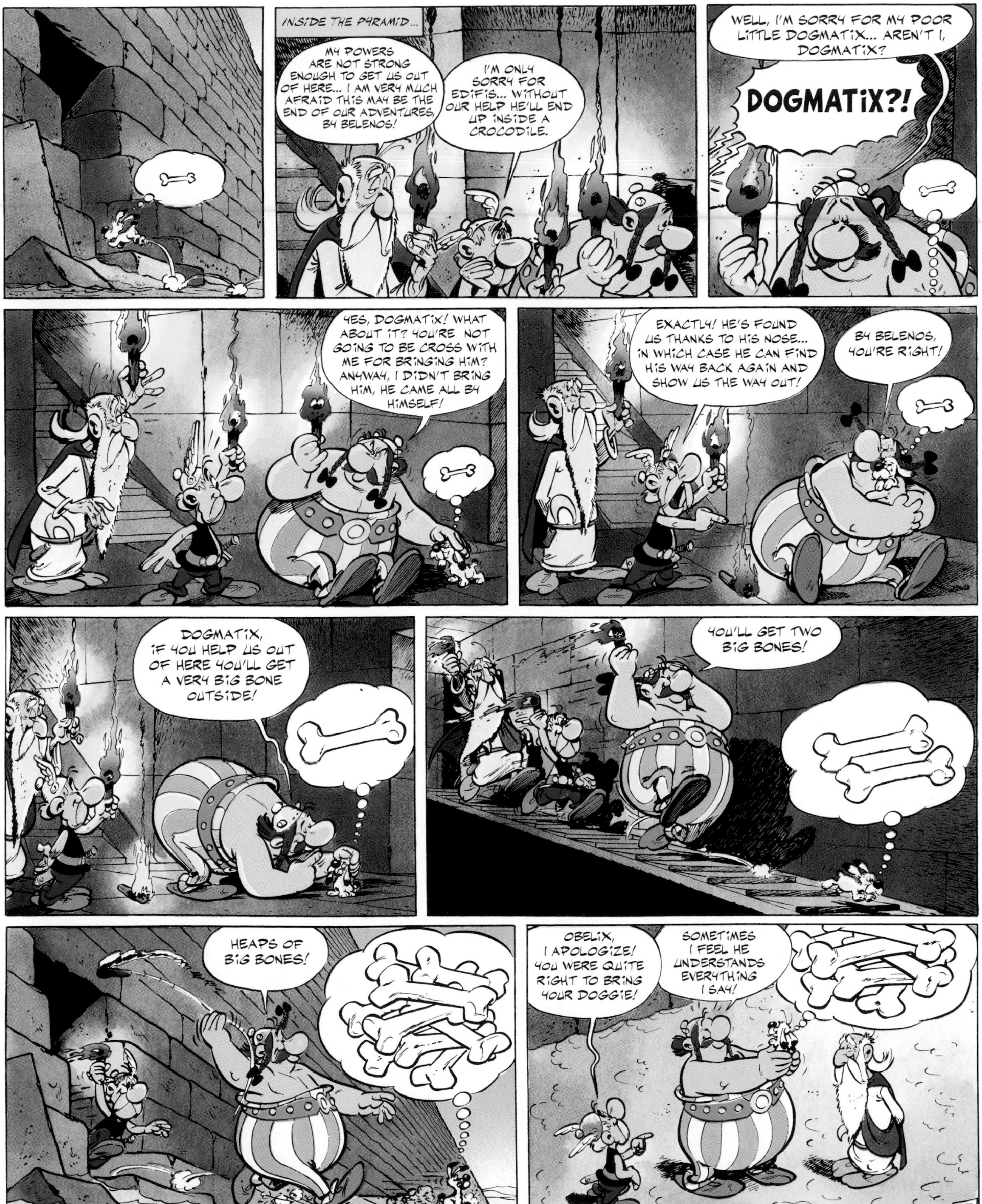
INSIDE THE PYRAMID...
MY POWERS ARE NOT STRONG ENOUGH TO GET US OUT OF HERE... I AM VERY MUCH AFRAID THIS MAY BE THE END OF OUR ADVENTURES, BY BELENOS!
I'M ONLY SORRY FOR EDIFIS... WITHOUT OUR HELP HE'LL END UP INSIDE A CROCODILE.
WELL, I'M SORRY FOR MY POOR LITTLE DOGMATIX... AREN'T I, DOGMATIX?
DOGMATIX?!
YES, DOGMATIX! WHAT ABOUT IT? YOU'RE NOT GOING TO BE CROSS WITH ME FOR BRINGING HIM? ANYWAY, I DIDN'T BRING HIM, HE CAME ALL BY HIMSELF!
EXACTLY! HE'S FOUND US THANKS TO HIS NOSE... IN WHICH CASE HE CAN FIND HIS WAY BACK AGAIN AND SHOW US THE WAY OUT!
BY BELENOS, YOU'RE RIGHT!
DOGMATIX, IF YOU HELP US OUT OF HERE YOU'LL GET A VERY BIG BONE OUTSIDE!
YOU'LL GET TWO BIG BONES!
HEAPS OF BIG BONES!
OBELIX, I APOLOGIZE! YOU WERE QUITE RIGHT TO BRING YOUR DOGGIE!
SOMETIMES I FEEL HE UNDERSTANDS EVERYTHING I SAY!

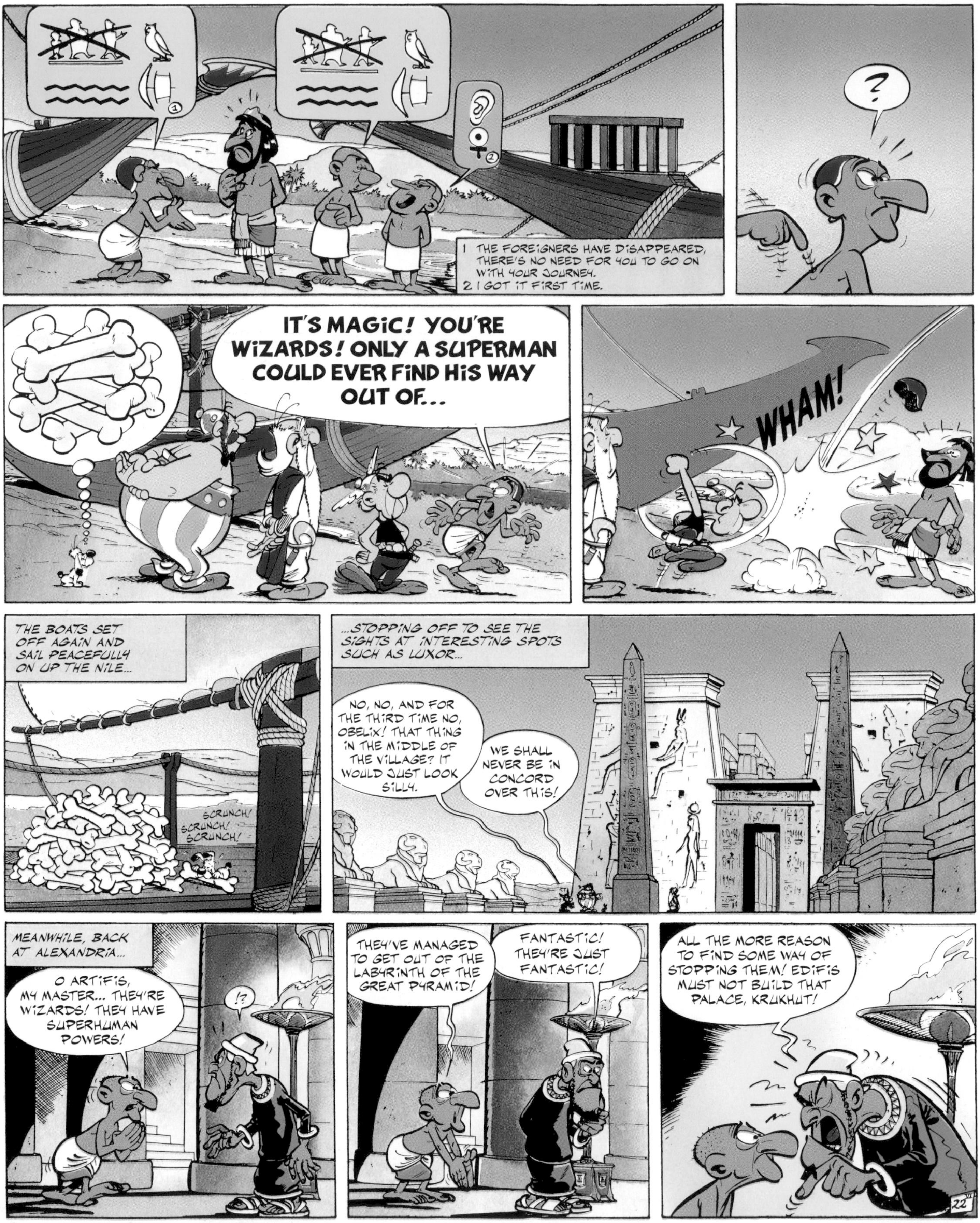
1 THE FOREIGNERS HAVE DISAPPEARED, THERE'S NO NEED FOR YOU TO GO ON WITH YOUR JOURNEY.
2 I GOT IT FIRST TIME.
?
IT'S MAGIC! YOU'RE WIZARDS! ONLY A SUPERMAN COULD EVER FIND HIS WAY OUT OF...
WHAM!
THE BOATS SET OFF AGAIN AND SAIL PEACEFULLY ON UP THE NILE...
SCRUNCH! SCRUNCH! SCRUNCH!
...STOPPING OFF TO SEE THE SIGHTS AT INTERESTING SPOTS SUCH AS LUXOR...
NO, NO, AND FOR THE THIRD TIME NO, OBELIX! THAT THING IN THE MIDDLE OF THE VILLAGE? IT WOULD JUST LOOK SILLY.
WE SHALL NEVER BE IN CONCORD OVER THIS!
MEANWHILE, BACK AT ALEXANDRIA...
O ARTIFIS, MY MASTER... THEY'RE WIZARDS! THEY HAVE SUPERHUMAN POWERS!
!?
THEY'VE MANAGED TO GET OUT OF THE LABYRINTH OF THE GREAT PYRAMID!
FANTASTIC! THEY'RE JUST FANTASTIC!
ALL THE MORE REASON TO FIND SOME WAY OF STOPPING THEM! EDIFIS MUST NOT BUILD THAT PALACE, KRUKHUT!

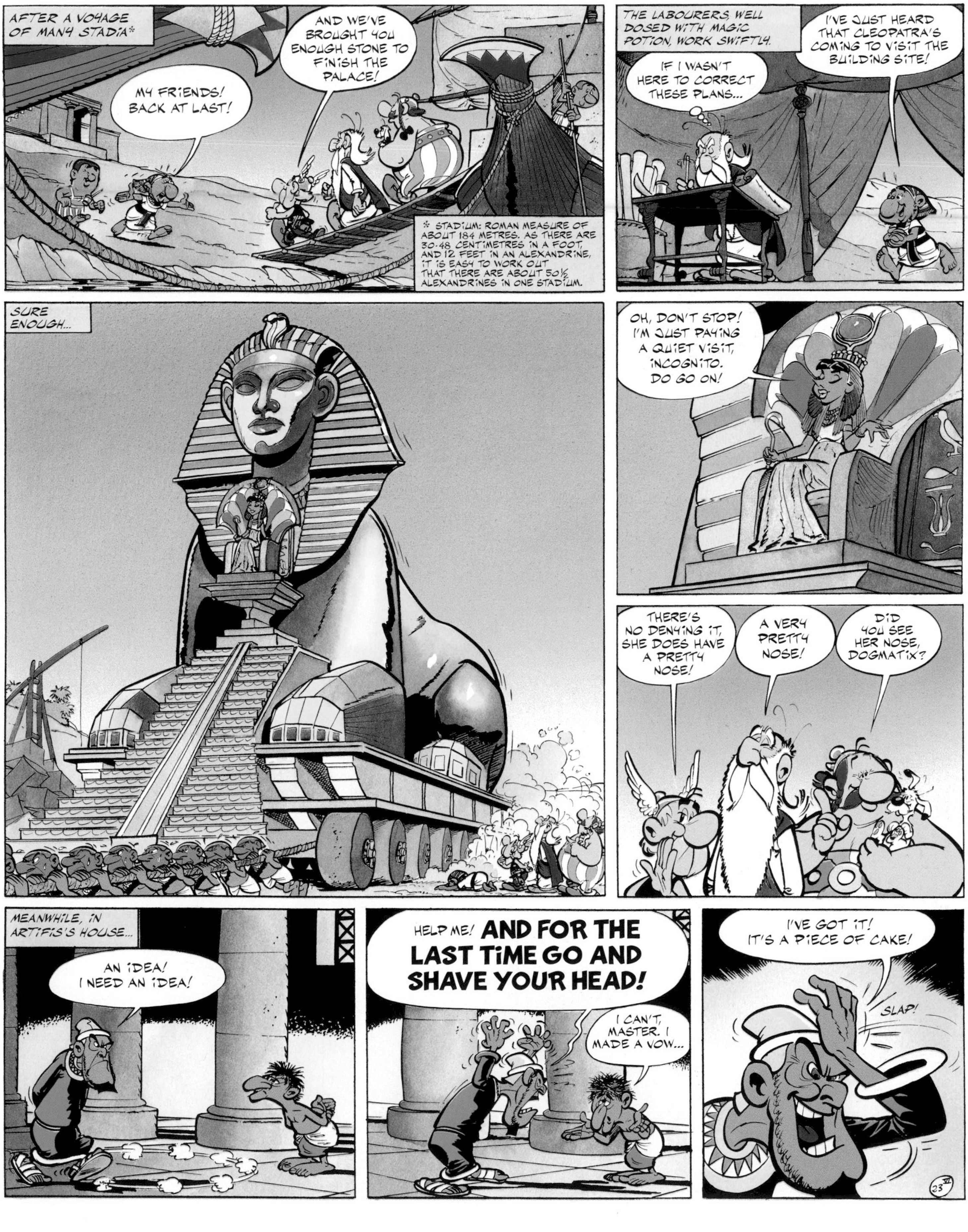

AFTER A VOYAGE OF MANY STADIA*
MY FRIENDS! BACK AT LAST!
AND WE'VE BROUGHT YOU ENOUGH STONE TO FINISH THE PALACE!
* STADIUM: ROMAN MEASURE OF ABOUT 184 METRES. AS THERE ARE 30.48 CENTIMETRES IN A FOOT, AND 12 FEET IN AN ALEXANDRINE, IT IS EASY TO WORK OUT THAT THERE ARE ABOUT 50½ ALEXANDRINES IN ONE STADIUM.
THE LABOURERS, WELL DOSED WITH MAGIC POTION, WORK SWIFTLY.
IF I WASN'T HERE TO CORRECT THESE PLANS...
I'VE JUST HEARD THAT CLEOPATRA'S COMING TO VISIT THE BUILDING SITE!
SURE ENOUGH...
OH, DON'T STOP! I'M JUST PAYING A QUIET VISIT, INCOGNITO. DO GO ON!
THERE'S NO DENYING IT, SHE DOES HAVE A PRETTY NOSE!
A VERY PRETTY NOSE!
DID YOU SEE HER NOSE, DOGMATIX?
MEANWHILE, IN ARTIFIS'S HOUSE...
AN IDEA! I NEED AN IDEA!
HELP ME! AND FOR THE LAST TIME GO AND SHAVE YOUR HEAD!
I CAN'T, MASTER. I MADE A VOW...
I'VE GOT IT! IT'S A PIECE OF CAKE!
SLAP!

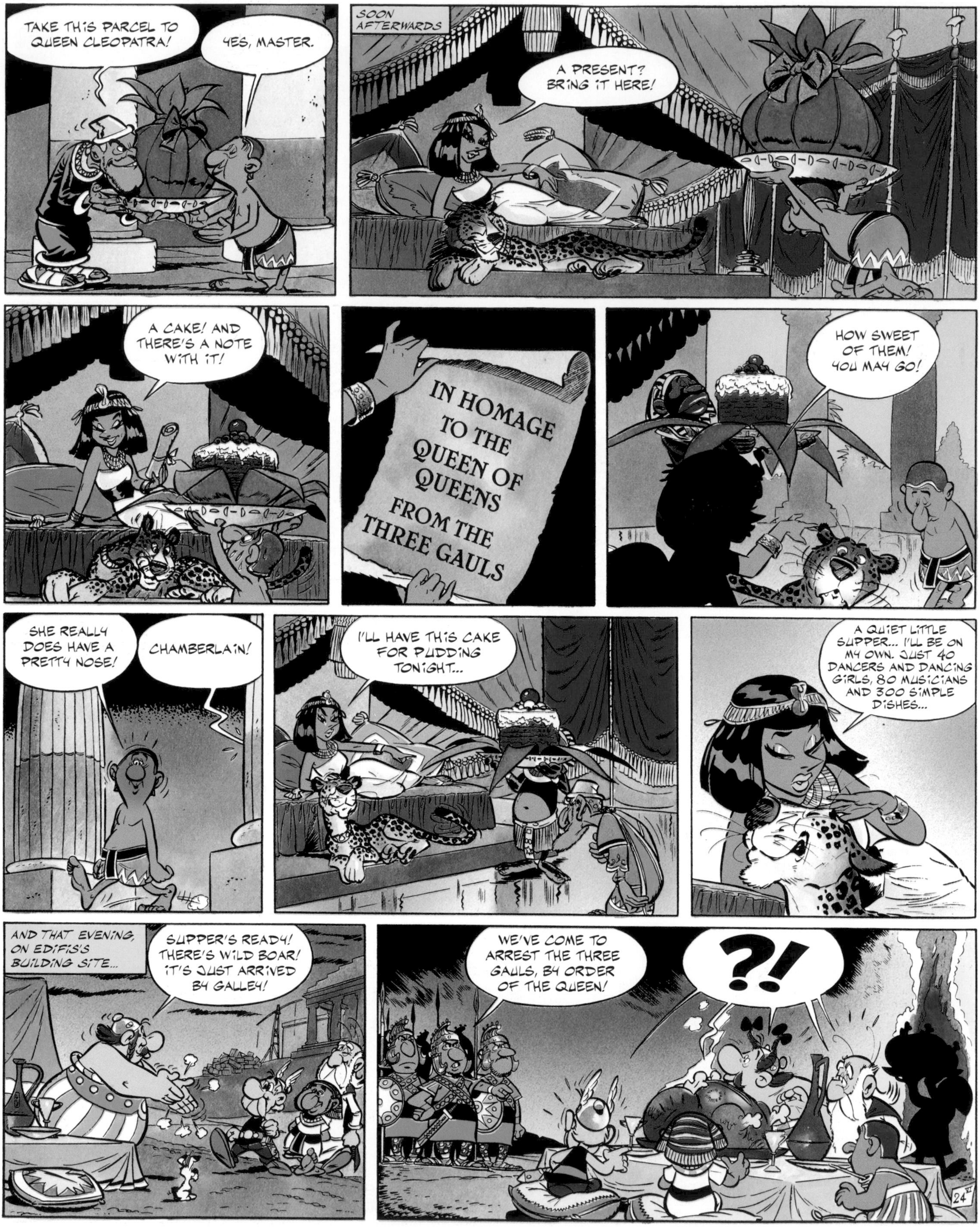
TAKE THIS PARCEL TO QUEEN CLEOPATRA!
YES, MASTER.
SOON AFTERWARDS
A PRESENT? BRING IT HERE!
A CAKE! AND THERE'S A NOTE WITH IT!
IN HOMAGE TO THE QUEEN OF QUEENS FROM THE THREE GAULS
HOW SWEET OF THEM! YOU MAY GO!
SHE REALLY DOES HAVE A PRETTY NOSE!
CHAMBERLAIN!
I'LL HAVE THIS CAKE FOR PUDDING TONIGHT...
A QUIET LITTLE SUPPER... I'LL BE ON MY OWN. JUST 40 DANCERS AND DANCING GIRLS, 80 MUSICIANS AND 300 SIMPLE DISHES...
AND THAT EVENING, ON EDIFIS'S BUILDING SITE...
SUPPER'S READY! THERE'S WILD BOAR! IT'S JUST ARRIVED BY GALLEY!
WE'VE COME TO ARREST THE THREE GAULS, BY ORDER OF THE QUEEN!
?!

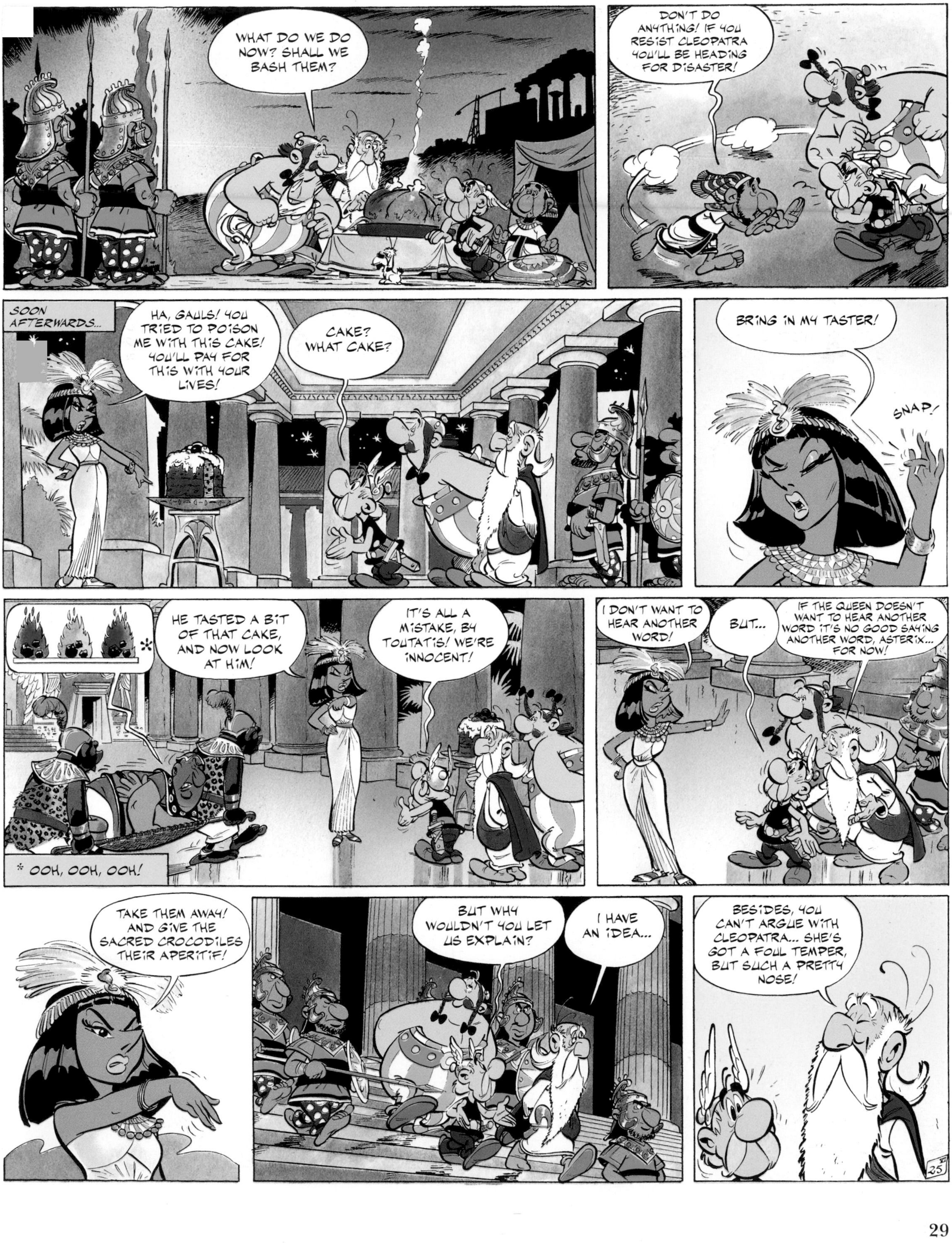
WHAT DO WE DO NOW? SHALL WE BASH THEM?
DON'T DO ANYTHING! IF YOU RESIST CLEOPATRA YOU'LL BE HEADING FOR DISASTER!
SOON AFTERWARDS...
HA, GAULS! YOU TRIED TO POISON ME WITH THIS CAKE! YOU'LL PAY FOR THIS WITH YOUR LIVES!
CAKE? WHAT CAKE?
BRING IN MY TASTER!
SNAP!
HE TASTED A BIT OF THAT CAKE, AND NOW LOOK AT HIM!
IT'S ALL A MISTAKE, BY TOUTATIS! WE'RE INNOCENT!
* OOH, OOH, OOH!
I DON'T WANT TO HEAR ANOTHER WORD!
BUT...
IF THE QUEEN DOESN'T WANT TO HEAR ANOTHER WORD IT'S NO GOOD SAYING ANOTHER WORD, ASTERIX... FOR NOW!
TAKE THEM AWAY! AND GIVE THE SACRED CROCODILES THEIR APERITIF!
BUT WHY WOULDN'T YOU LET US EXPLAIN?
I HAVE AN IDEA...
BESIDES, YOU CAN'T ARGUE WITH CLEOPATRA... SHE'S GOT A FOUL TEMPER, BUT SUCH A PRETTY NOSE!

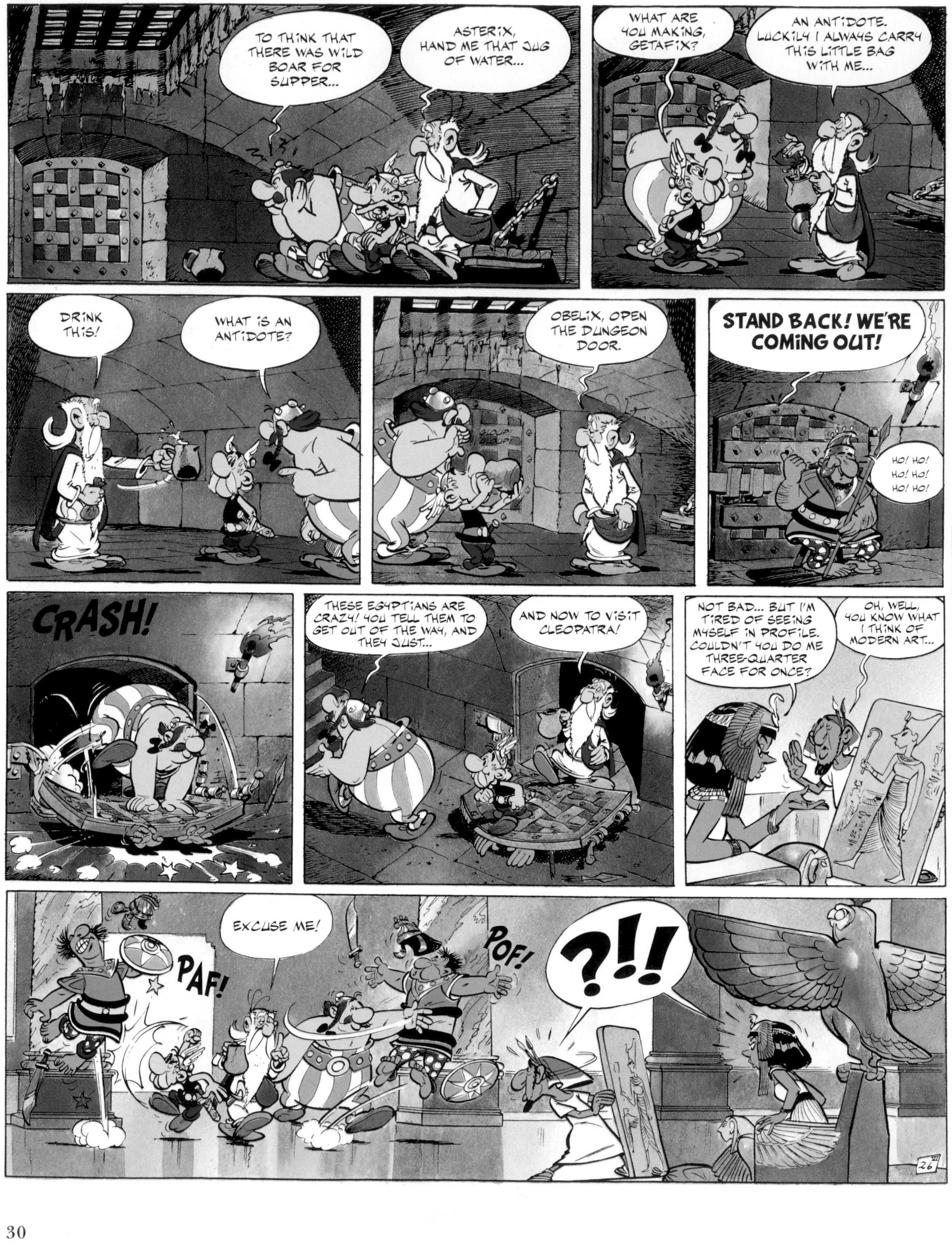

TO THINK THAT THERE WAS WILD BOAR FOR SUPPER...
ASTERIX, HAND ME THAT JUG OF WATER...
WHAT ARE YOU MAKING, GETAFIX?
AN ANTIDOTE. LUCKILY I ALWAYS CARRY THIS LITTLE BAG WITH ME...
DRINK THIS!
WHAT IS AN ANTIDOTE?
OBELIX, OPEN THE DUNGEON DOOR.
STAND BACK! WE'RE COMING OUT!
HO! HO! HO! HO! HO! HO!
CRASH!
THESE EGYPTIANS ARE CRAZY! YOU TELL THEM TO GET OUT OF THE WAY, AND THEY JUST...
AND NOW TO VISIT CLEOPATRA!
NOT BAD... BUT I'M TIRED OF SEEING MYSELF IN PROFILE. COULDN'T YOU DO ME THREE-QUARTER FACE FOR ONCE?
OH, WELL, YOU KNOW WHAT I THINK OF MODERN ART...
EXCUSE ME!
PAF!
POF!
?!!
26

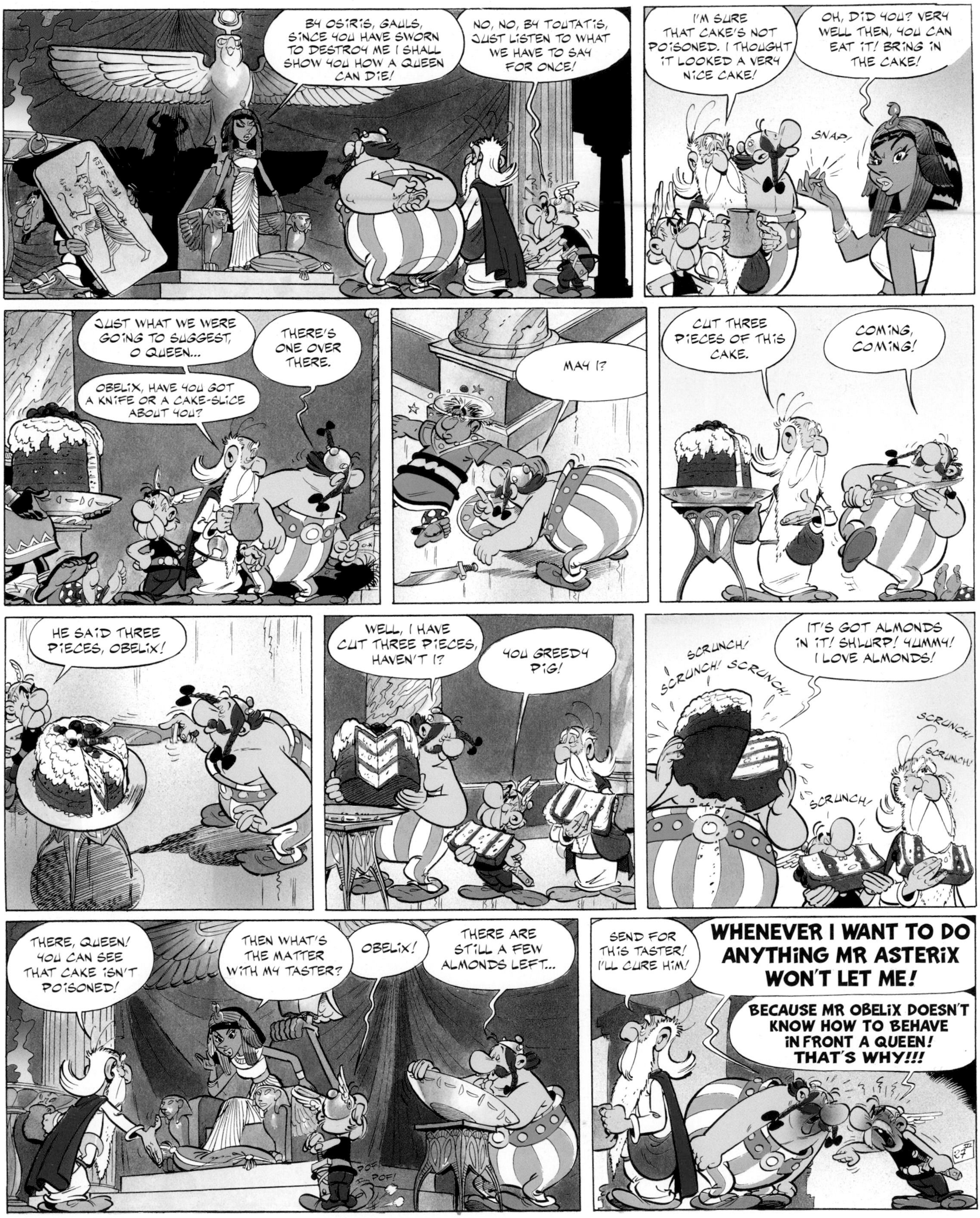

BY OSIRIS, GAULS, SINCE YOU HAVE SWORN TO DESTROY ME I SHALL SHOW YOU HOW A QUEEN CAN DIE!
NO, NO, BY TOUTATIS, JUST LISTEN TO WHAT WE HAVE TO SAY FOR ONCE!
I'M SURE THAT CAKE'S NOT POISONED. I THOUGHT IT LOOKED A VERY NICE CAKE!
OH, DID YOU? VERY WELL THEN, YOU CAN EAT IT! BRING IN THE CAKE!
SNAP!
JUST WHAT WE WERE GOING TO SUGGEST, O QUEEN...
OBELIX, HAVE YOU GOT A KNIFE OR A CAKE-SLICE ABOUT YOU?
THERE'S ONE OVER THERE.
MAY I?
CUT THREE PIECES OF THIS CAKE.
COMING, COMING!
HE SAID THREE PIECES, OBELIX!
WELL, I HAVE CUT THREE PIECES, HAVEN'T I?
YOU GREEDY PIG!
SCRUNCH! SCRUNCH! SCRUNCH!
IT'S GOT ALMONDS IN IT! SHLURP! YUMMY! I LOVE ALMONDS!
SCRUNCH! SCRUNCH!
SCRUNCH!
THERE, QUEEN! YOU CAN SEE THAT CAKE ISN'T POISONED!
THEN WHAT'S THE MATTER WITH MY TASTER?
OBELIX!
THERE ARE STILL A FEW ALMONDS LEFT...
POF! POF!
SEND FOR THIS TASTER! I'LL CURE HIM!
WHENEVER I WANT TO DO ANYTHING MR ASTERIX WON'T LET ME!
BECAUSE MR OBELIX DOESN'T KNOW HOW TO BEHAVE IN FRONT A QUEEN! THAT'S WHY!!!

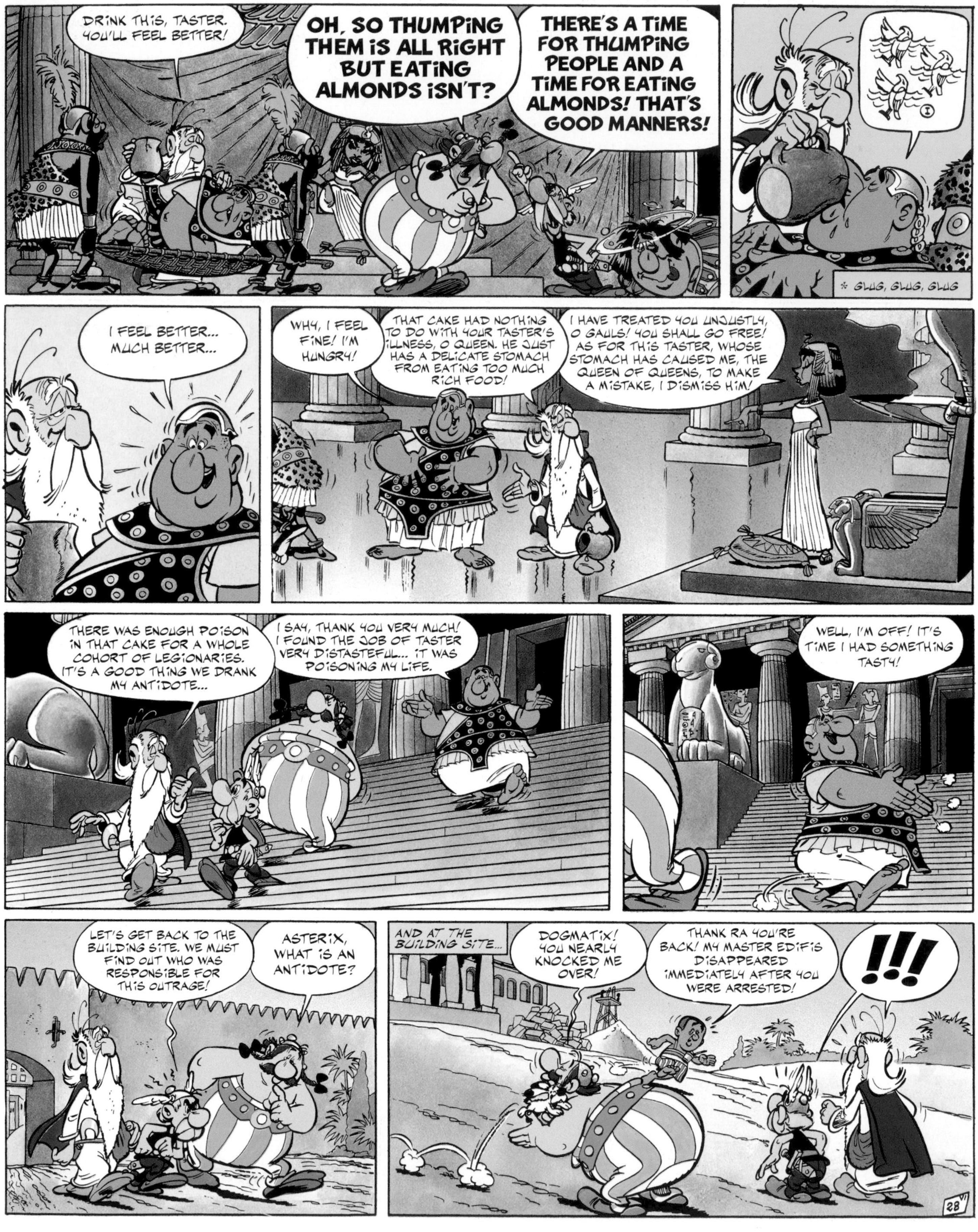
DRINK THIS, TASTER. YOU'LL FEEL BETTER!
OH, SO THUMPING THEM IS ALL RIGHT BUT EATING ALMONDS ISN'T?
THERE'S A TIME FOR THUMPING PEOPLE AND A TIME FOR EATING ALMONDS! THAT'S GOOD MANNERS!
* GLUG, GLUG, GLUG
I FEEL BETTER... MUCH BETTER...
WHY, I FEEL FINE! I'M HUNGRY!
THAT CAKE HAD NOTHING TO DO WITH YOUR TASTER'S ILLNESS, O QUEEN. HE JUST HAS A DELICATE STOMACH FROM EATING TOO MUCH RICH FOOD!
I HAVE TREATED YOU UNJUSTLY, O GAULS! YOU SHALL GO FREE! AS FOR THIS TASTER, WHOSE STOMACH HAS CAUSED ME, THE QUEEN OF QUEENS, TO MAKE A MISTAKE, I DISMISS HIM!
THERE WAS ENOUGH POISON IN THAT CAKE FOR A WHOLE COHORT OF LEGIONARIES. IT'S A GOOD THING WE DRANK MY ANTIDOTE...
I SAY, THANK YOU VERY MUCH! I FOUND THE JOB OF TASTER VERY DISTASTEFUL... IT WAS POISONING MY LIFE.
WELL, I'M OFF! IT'S TIME I HAD SOMETHING TASTY!
LET'S GET BACK TO THE BUILDING SITE. WE MUST FIND OUT WHO WAS RESPONSIBLE FOR THIS OUTRAGE!
ASTERIX, WHAT IS AN ANTIDOTE?
AND AT THE BUILDING SITE...
DOGMATIX! YOU NEARLY KNOCKED ME OVER!
THANK RA YOU'RE BACK! MY MASTER EDIFIS DISAPPEARED IMMEDIATELY AFTER YOU WERE ARRESTED!
!!!
28

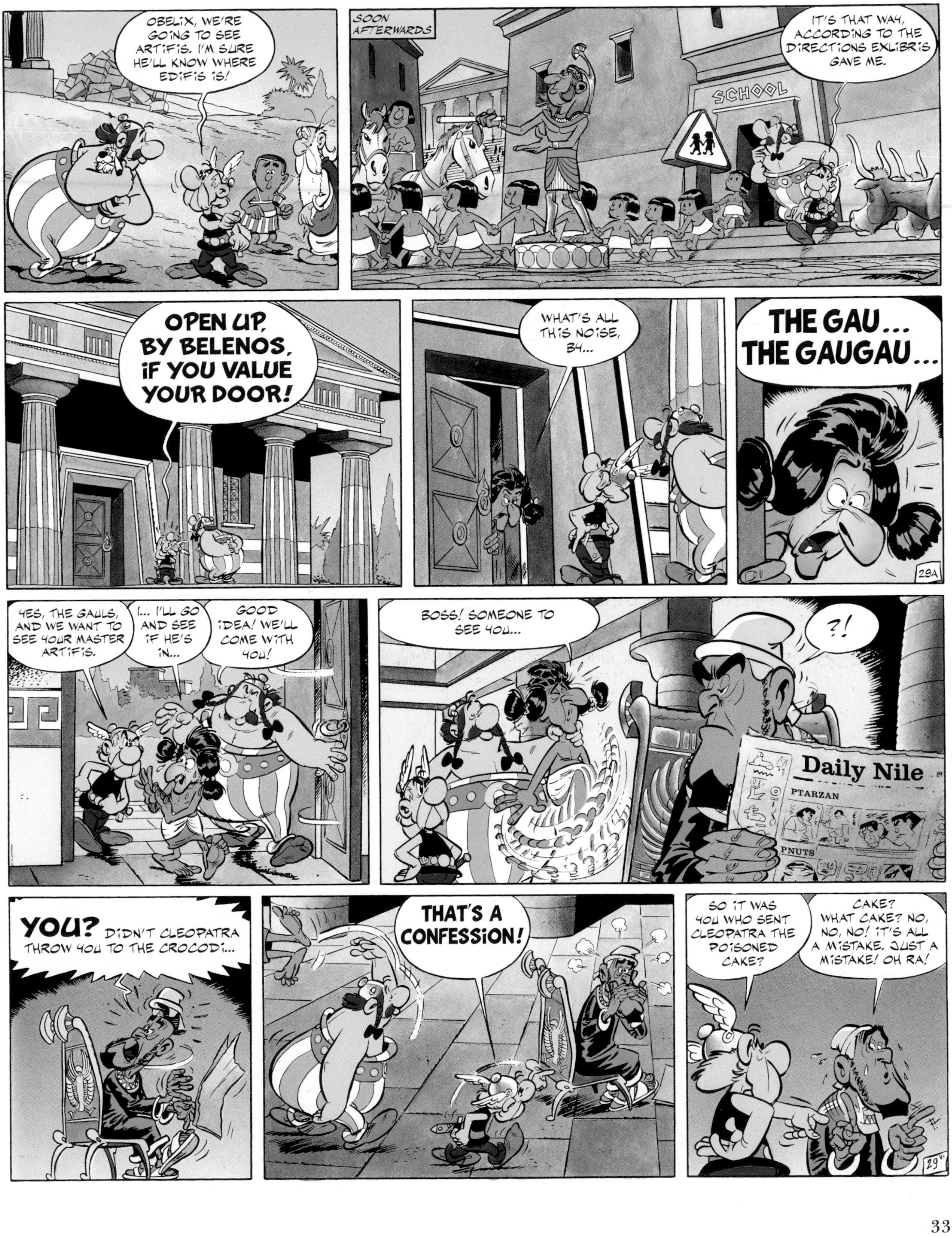
OBELIX, WE'RE GOING TO SEE ARTIFIS. I'M SURE HE'LL KNOW WHERE EDIFIS IS!
SOON AFTERWARDS
SCHOOL
IT'S THAT WAY, ACCORDING TO THE DIRECTIONS EXLIBRIS GAVE ME.
OPEN UP, BY BELENOS, IF YOU VALUE YOUR DOOR!
WHAT'S ALL THIS NOISE, BY...
THE GAU... THE GAUGAU...
YES, THE GAULS, AND WE WANT TO SEE YOUR MASTER ARTIFIS.
I... I'LL GO AND SEE IF HE'S IN...
GOOD IDEA! WE'LL COME WITH YOU!
BOSS! SOMEONE TO SEE YOU...
?!
Daily Nile
PTARZAN
PNUTS
YOU? DIDN'T CLEOPATRA THROW YOU TO THE CROCODI...
THAT'S A CONFESSION!
SO IT WAS YOU WHO SENT CLEOPATRA THE POISONED CAKE?
CAKE? WHAT CAKE? NO, NO, NO! IT'S ALL A MISTAKE. JUST A MISTAKE! OH RA!

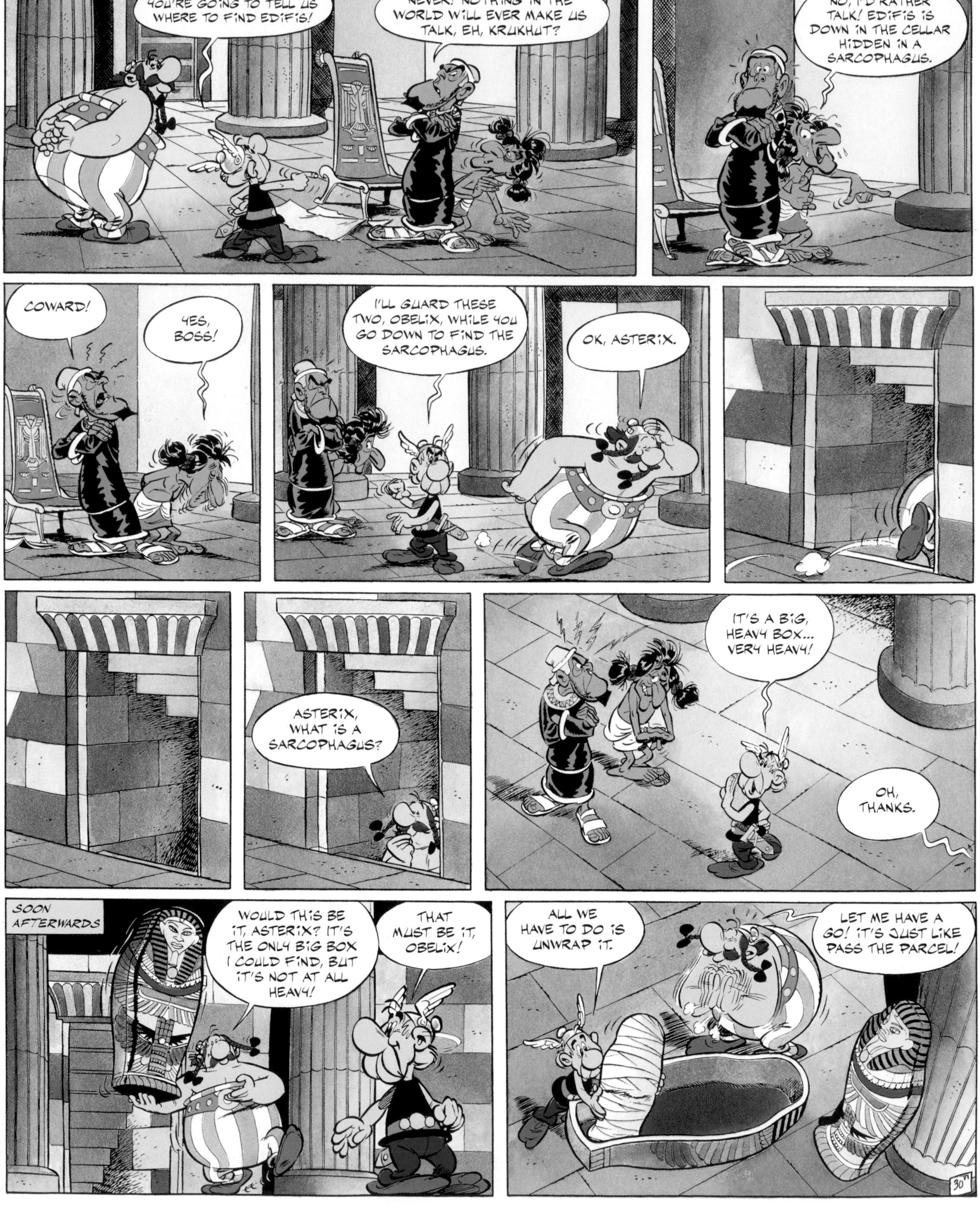
YOU'RE GOING TO TELL US WHERE TO FIND EDIFIS!
NEVER! NOTHING IN THE WORLD WILL EVER MAKE US TALK, EH, KRUKHUT?
NO, I'D RATHER TALK! EDIFIS IS DOWN IN THE CELLAR HIDDEN IN A SARCOPHAGUS.
COWARD!
YES, BOSS!
I'LL GUARD THESE TWO, OBELIX, WHILE YOU GO DOWN TO FIND THE SARCOPHAGUS.
OK, ASTERIX.
ASTERIX, WHAT IS A SARCOPHAGUS?
IT'S A BIG, HEAVY BOX... VERY HEAVY!
OH, THANKS.
SOON AFTERWARDS
WOULD THIS BE IT, ASTERIX? IT'S THE ONLY BIG BOX I COULD FIND, BUT IT'S NOT AT ALL HEAVY!
THAT MUST BE IT, OBELIX!
ALL WE HAVE TO DO IS UNWRAP IT.
LET ME HAVE A GO! IT'S JUST LIKE PASS THE PARCEL!

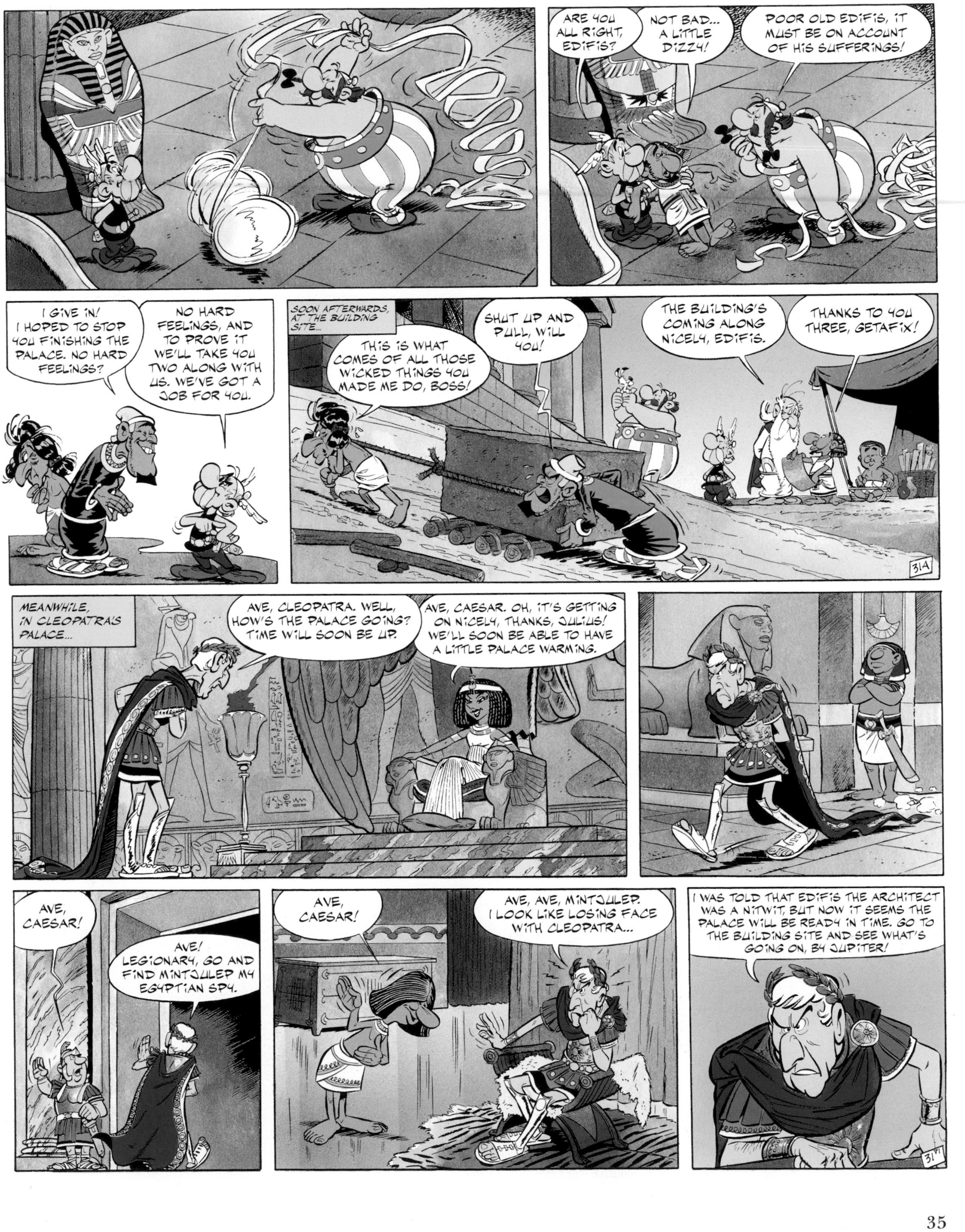

ARE YOU ALL RIGHT, EDIFIS?
NOT BAD... A LITTLE DIZZY!
POOR OLD EDIFIS, IT MUST BE ON ACCOUNT OF HIS SUFFERINGS!
I GIVE IN! I HOPED TO STOP YOU FINISHING THE PALACE. NO HARD FEELINGS?
NO HARD FEELINGS, AND TO PROVE IT WE'LL TAKE YOU TWO ALONG WITH US. WE'VE GOT A JOB FOR YOU.
SOON AFTERWARDS, AT THE BUILDING SITE...
THIS IS WHAT COMES OF ALL THOSE WICKED THINGS YOU MADE ME DO, BOSS!
SHUT UP AND PULL, WILL YOU!
THE BUILDING'S COMING ALONG NICELY, EDIFIS.
THANKS TO YOU THREE, GETAFIX!
MEANWHILE, IN CLEOPATRA'S PALACE...
AVE, CLEOPATRA. WELL, HOW'S THE PALACE GOING? TIME WILL SOON BE UP.
AVE, CAESAR. OH, IT'S GETTING ON NICELY, THANKS, JULIUS! WE'LL SOON BE ABLE TO HAVE A LITTLE PALACE WARMING.
AVE, CAESAR!
AVE! LEGIONARY, GO AND FIND MINTJULEP MY EGYPTIAN SPY.
AVE, CAESAR!
AVE, AVE, MINTJULEP. I LOOK LIKE LOSING FACE WITH CLEOPATRA...
I WAS TOLD THAT EDIFIS THE ARCHITECT WAS A NITWIT, BUT NOW IT SEEMS THE PALACE WILL BE READY IN TIME. GO TO THE BUILDING SITE AND SEE WHAT'S GOING ON, BY JUPITER!

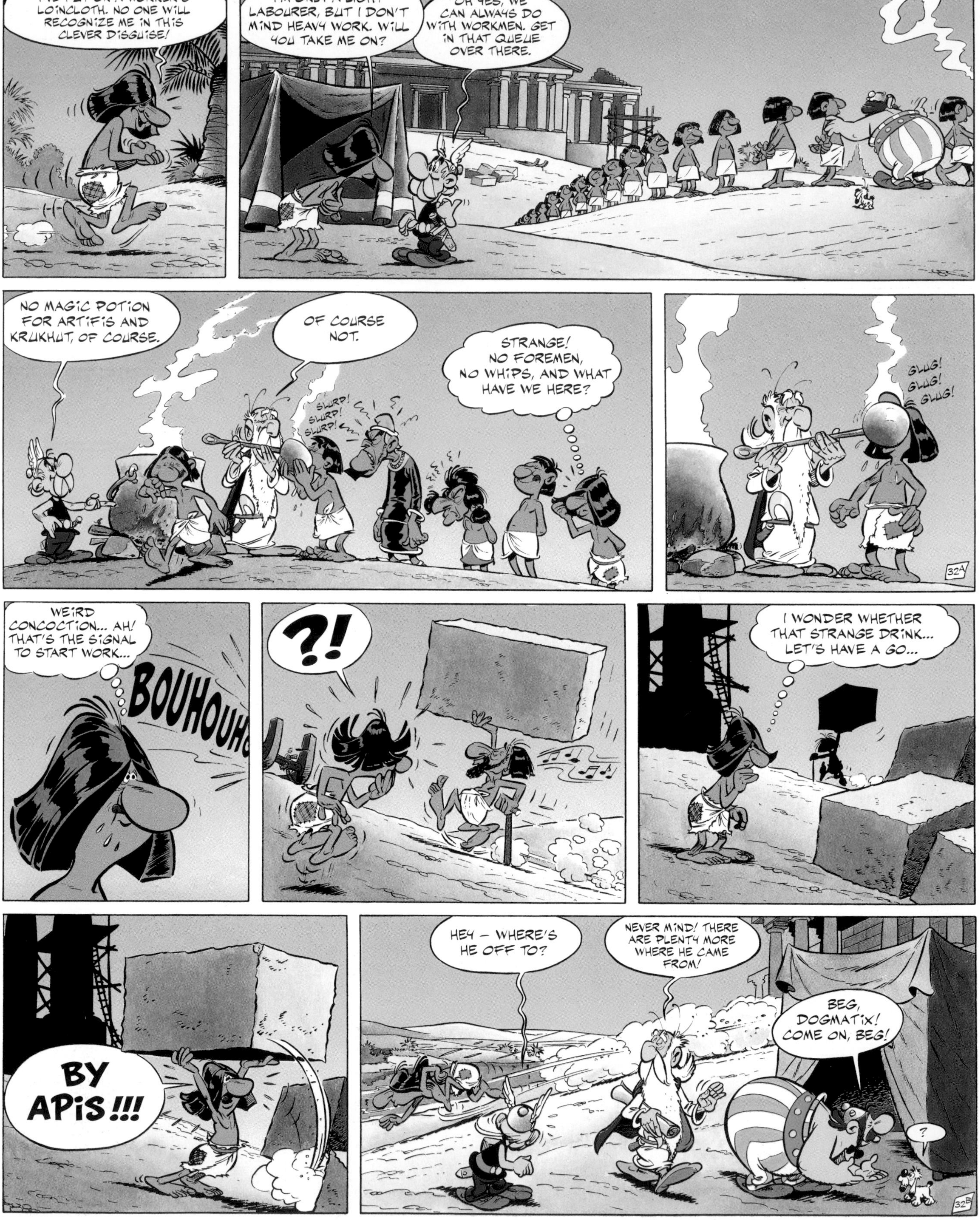

I'VE PUT ON A WORKER'S LOINCLOTH. NO ONE WILL RECOGNIZE ME IN THIS CLEVER DISGUISE!
I'M ONLY A LIGHT LABOURER, BUT I DON'T MIND HEAVY WORK. WILL YOU TAKE ME ON?
OH YES, WE CAN ALWAYS DO WITH WORKMEN. GET IN THAT QUEUE OVER THERE.
NO MAGIC POTION FOR ARTIFIS AND KRUKHUT, OF COURSE.
OF COURSE NOT.
SLURP! SLURP! SLURP!
STRANGE! NO FOREMEN, NO WHIPS, AND WHAT HAVE WE HERE?
GLUG! GLUG! GLUG!
32A
WEIRD CONCOCTION... AH! THAT'S THE SIGNAL TO START WORK...
BOUHOUHO
?!
I WONDER WHETHER THAT STRANGE DRINK... LET'S HAVE A GO...
BY APIS!!!
HEY – WHERE'S HE OFF TO?
NEVER MIND! THERE ARE PLENTY MORE WHERE HE CAME FROM!
BEG, DOGMATIX! COME ON, BEG!
?
32B

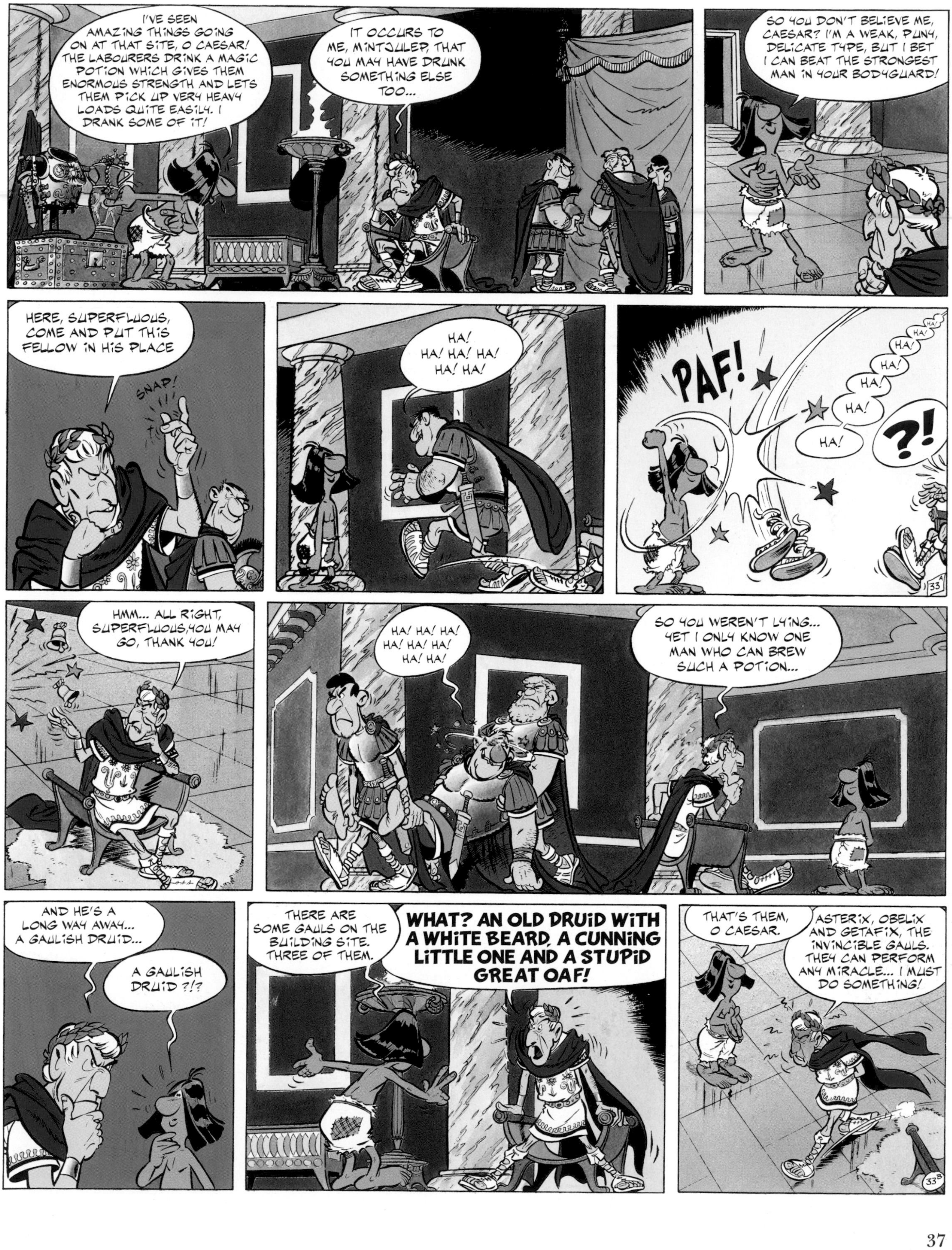
I'VE SEEN AMAZING THINGS GOING ON AT THAT SITE, O CAESAR! THE LABOURERS DRINK A MAGIC POTION WHICH GIVES THEM ENORMOUS STRENGTH AND LETS THEM PICK UP VERY HEAVY LOADS QUITE EASILY. I DRANK SOME OF IT!
IT OCCURS TO ME, MINTJULEP, THAT YOU MAY HAVE DRUNK SOMETHING ELSE TOO...
SO YOU DON'T BELIEVE ME, CAESAR? I'M A WEAK, PUNY, DELICATE TYPE, BUT I BET I CAN BEAT THE STRONGEST MAN IN YOUR BODYGUARD!
HERE, SUPERFLUOUS, COME AND PUT THIS FELLOW IN HIS PLACE
SNAP!
HA! HA! HA! HA! HA! HA!
PAF!
HA! HA! HA! HA! HA! HA! HA!
?!
33A
HMM... ALL RIGHT, SUPERFLUOUS, YOU MAY GO, THANK YOU!
HA! HA! HA! HA! HA! HA! HA! HA!
SO YOU WEREN'T LYING... YET I ONLY KNOW ONE MAN WHO CAN BREW SUCH A POTION...
AND HE'S A LONG WAY AWAY... A GAULISH DRUID...
A GAULISH DRUID ?!?
THERE ARE SOME GAULS ON THE BUILDING SITE. THREE OF THEM.
WHAT? AN OLD DRUID WITH A WHITE BEARD, A CUNNING LITTLE ONE AND A STUPID GREAT OAF!
THAT'S THEM, O CAESAR.
ASTERIX, OBELIX AND GETAFIX, THE INVINCIBLE GAULS. THEY CAN PERFORM ANY MIRACLE... I MUST DO SOMETHING!
33B

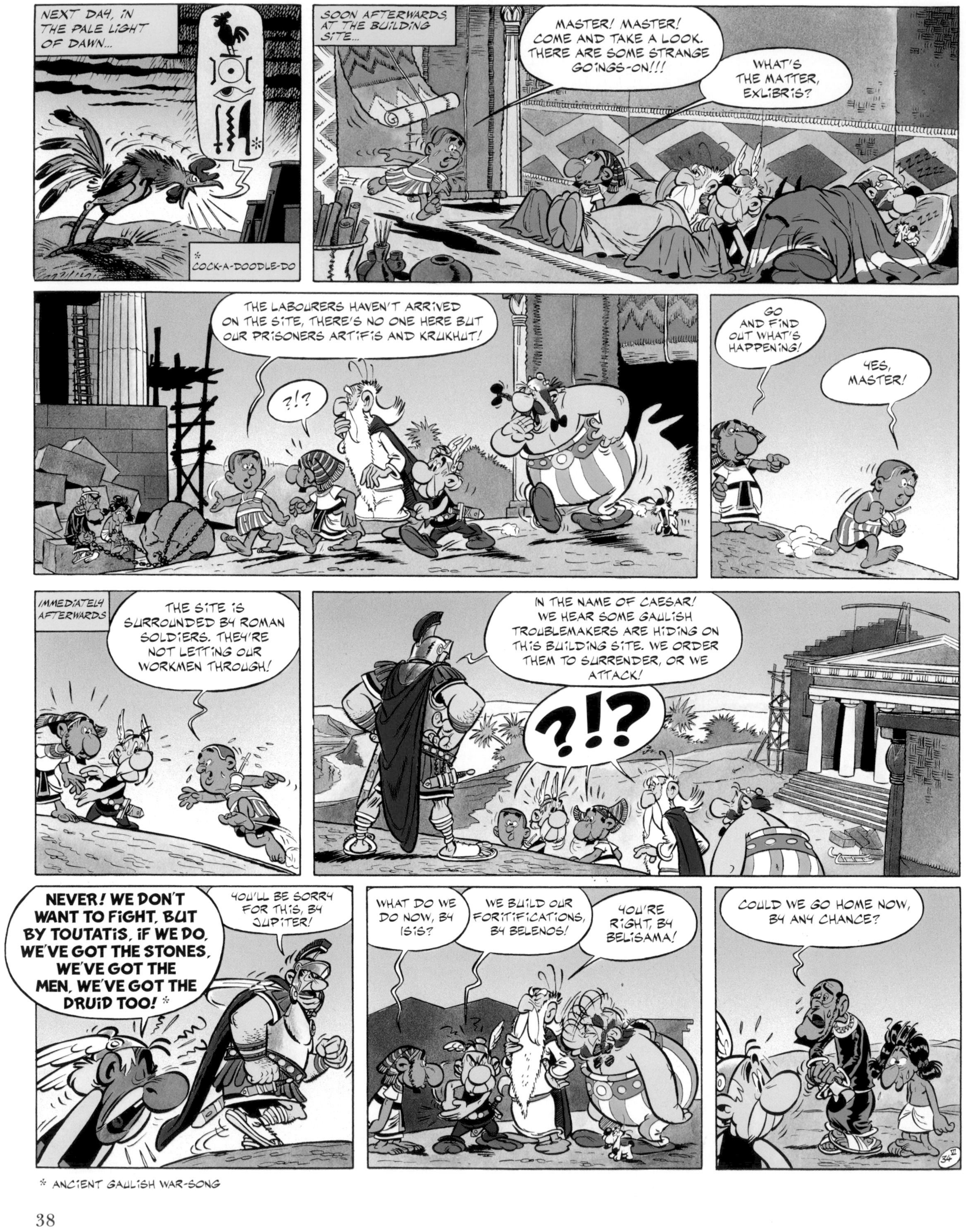
NEXT DAY, IN THE PALE LIGHT OF DAWN...
*
COCK-A-DOODLE-DO
SOON AFTERWARDS, AT THE BUILDING SITE...
MASTER! MASTER! COME AND TAKE A LOOK. THERE ARE SOME STRANGE GOINGS-ON!!!
WHAT'S THE MATTER, EXLIBRIS?
THE LABOURERS HAVEN'T ARRIVED ON THE SITE, THERE'S NO ONE HERE BUT OUR PRISONERS ARTIFIS AND KRUKHUT!
?!?
GO AND FIND OUT WHAT'S HAPPENING!
YES, MASTER!
IMMEDIATELY AFTERWARDS
THE SITE IS SURROUNDED BY ROMAN SOLDIERS. THEY'RE NOT LETTING OUR WORKMEN THROUGH!
IN THE NAME OF CAESAR! WE HEAR SOME GAULISH TROUBLEMAKERS ARE HIDING ON THIS BUILDING SITE. WE ORDER THEM TO SURRENDER, OR WE ATTACK!
?!?
NEVER! WE DON'T WANT TO FIGHT, BUT BY TOUTATIS, IF WE DO, WE'VE GOT THE STONES, WE'VE GOT THE MEN, WE'VE GOT THE DRUID TOO! *
YOU'LL BE SORRY FOR THIS, BY JUPITER!
WHAT DO WE DO NOW, BY ISIS?
WE BUILD OUR FORTIFICATIONS, BY BELENOS!
YOU'RE RIGHT, BY BELISAMA!
COULD WE GO HOME NOW, BY ANY CHANCE?

* ANCIENT GAULISH WAR-SONG

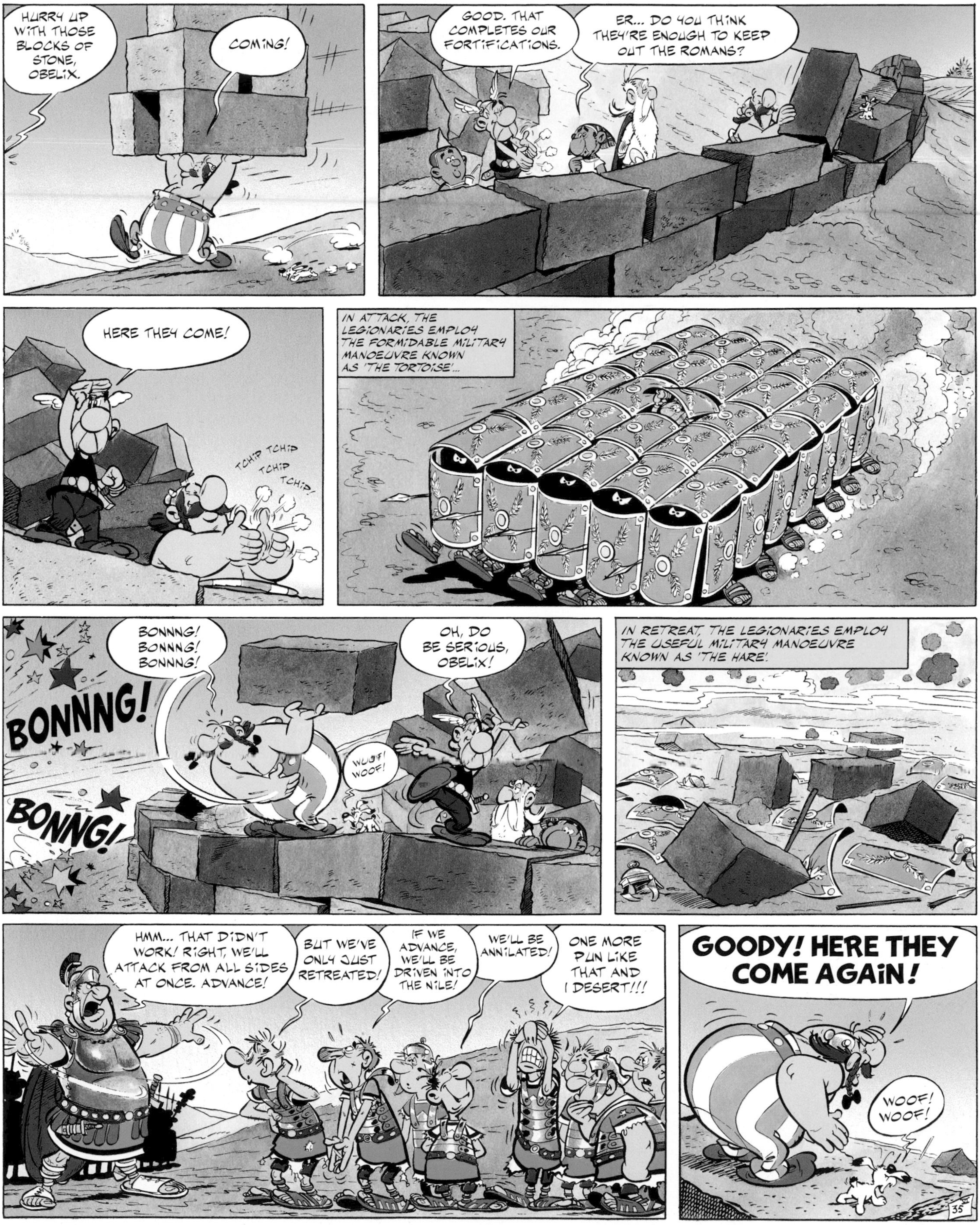
HURRY UP WITH THOSE BLOCKS OF STONE, OBELIX.
COMING!
GOOD. THAT COMPLETES OUR FORTIFICATIONS.
ER... DO YOU THINK THEY'RE ENOUGH TO KEEP OUT THE ROMANS?
HERE THEY COME!
TCHIP TCHIP TCHIP TCHIP!
IN ATTACK, THE LEGIONARIES EMPLOY THE FORMIDABLE MILITARY MANOEUVRE KNOWN AS 'THE TORTOISE'...
BONNNG! BONNNG! BONNNG!
OH, DO BE SERIOUS, OBELIX!
BONNNG!
WUFF! WOOF!
BONNG!
IN RETREAT, THE LEGIONARIES EMPLOY THE USEFUL MILITARY MANOEUVRE KNOWN AS 'THE HARE'.
HMM... THAT DIDN'T WORK! RIGHT, WE'LL ATTACK FROM ALL SIDES AT ONCE. ADVANCE!
BUT WE'VE ONLY JUST RETREATED!
IF WE ADVANCE, WE'LL BE DRIVEN INTO THE NILE!
WE'LL BE ANNILATED!
ONE MORE PUN LIKE THAT AND I DESERT!!!
GOODY! HERE THEY COME AGAIN!
WOOF! WOOF!

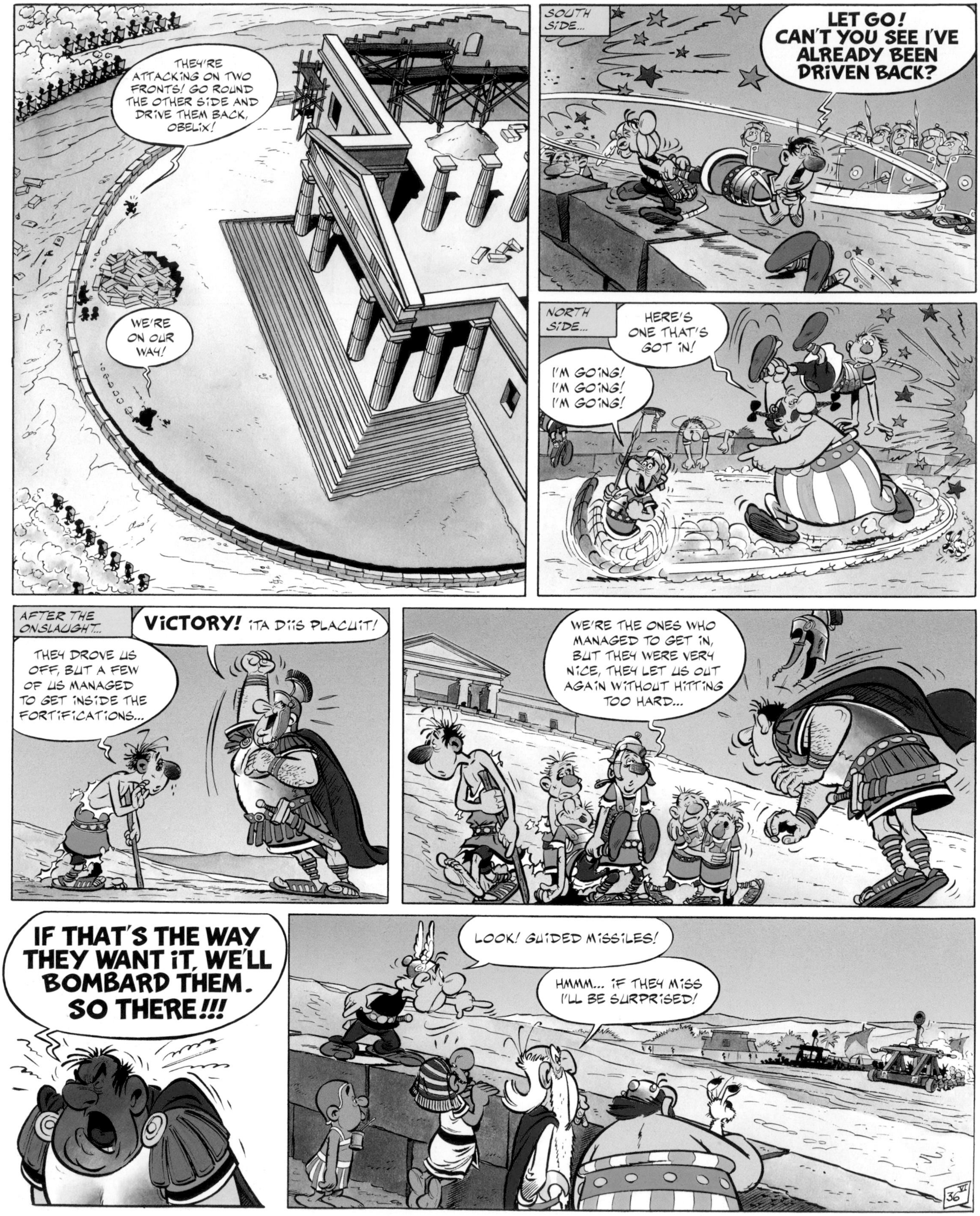
THEY'RE ATTACKING ON TWO FRONTS! GO ROUND THE OTHER SIDE AND DRIVE THEM BACK, OBELIX!
WE'RE ON OUR WAY!
SOUTH SIDE...
LET GO! CAN'T YOU SEE I'VE ALREADY BEEN DRIVEN BACK?
NORTH SIDE...
HERE'S ONE THAT'S GOT IN!
I'M GOING! I'M GOING! I'M GOING!
AFTER THE ONSLAUGHT...
VICTORY! ITA DIIS PLACUIT!
THEY DROVE US OFF, BUT A FEW OF US MANAGED TO GET INSIDE THE FORTIFICATIONS...
WE'RE THE ONES WHO MANAGED TO GET IN, BUT THEY WERE VERY NICE, THEY LET US OUT AGAIN WITHOUT HITTING TOO HARD...
IF THAT'S THE WAY THEY WANT IT, WE'LL BOMBARD THEM. SO THERE!!!
LOOK! GUIDED MISSILES!
HMMM... IF THEY MISS I'LL BE SURPRISED!
36 VI

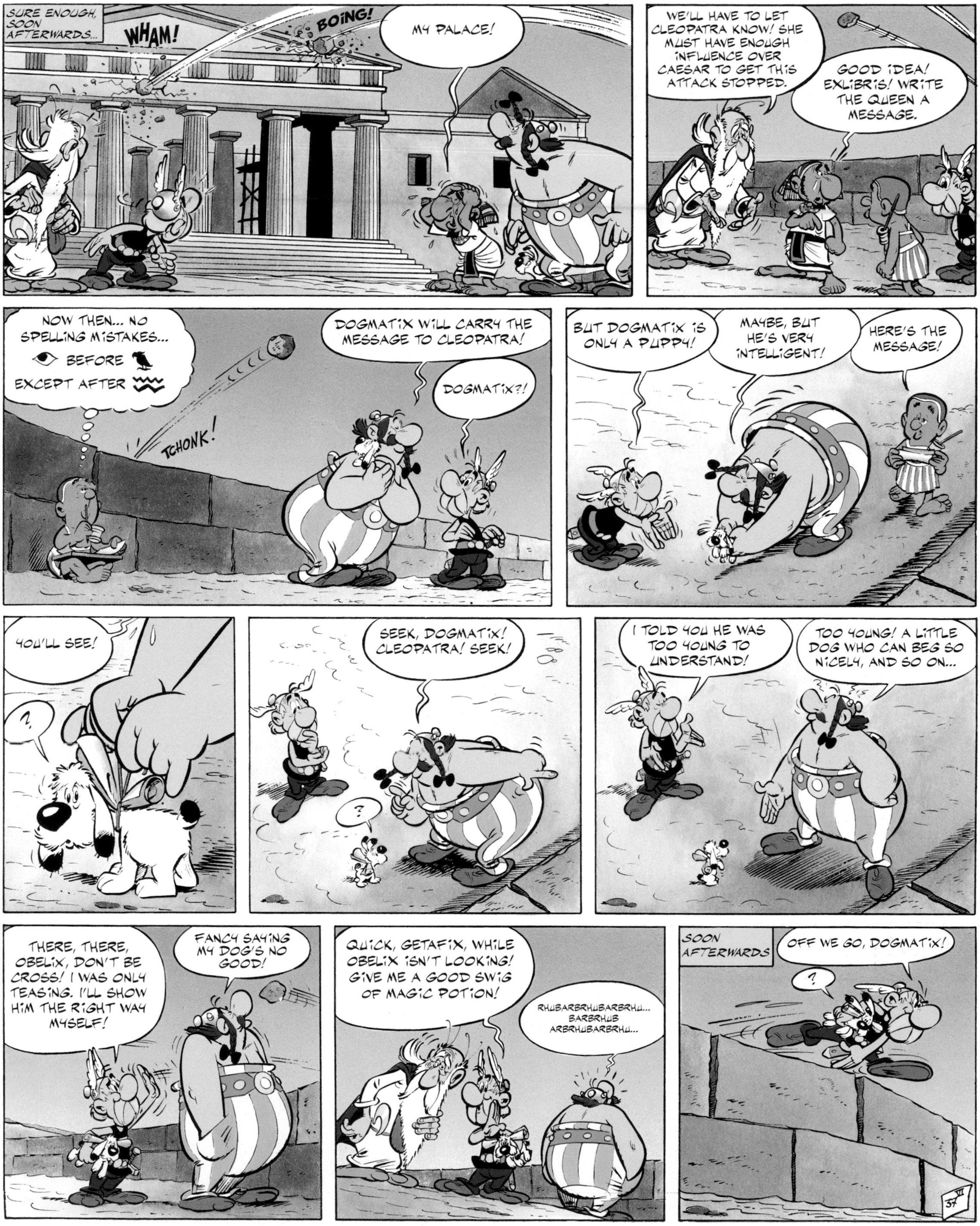
SURE ENOUGH, SOON AFTERWARDS...
WHAM!
BOING!
MY PALACE!
WE'LL HAVE TO LET CLEOPATRA KNOW! SHE MUST HAVE ENOUGH INFLUENCE OVER CAESAR TO GET THIS ATTACK STOPPED.
GOOD IDEA! EXLIBRIS! WRITE THE QUEEN A MESSAGE.
NOW THEN... NO SPELLING MISTAKES...
BEFORE
EXCEPT AFTER
TCHONK!
DOGMATIX WILL CARRY THE MESSAGE TO CLEOPATRA!
DOGMATIX?!
BUT DOGMATIX IS ONLY A PUPPY!
MAYBE, BUT HE'S VERY INTELLIGENT!
HERE'S THE MESSAGE!
YOU'LL SEE!
?
SEEK, DOGMATIX! CLEOPATRA! SEEK!
?
I TOLD YOU HE WAS TOO YOUNG TO UNDERSTAND!
TOO YOUNG! A LITTLE DOG WHO CAN BEG SO NICELY, AND SO ON...
THERE, THERE, OBELIX, DON'T BE CROSS! I WAS ONLY TEASING. I'LL SHOW HIM THE RIGHT WAY MYSELF!
FANCY SAYING MY DOG'S NO GOOD!
QUICK, GETAFIX, WHILE OBELIX ISN'T LOOKING! GIVE ME A GOOD SWIG OF MAGIC POTION!
RHUBARBRHUBARBRHU... BARBRHUB ARBRHUBARBRHU...
SOON AFTERWARDS
OFF WE GO, DOGMATIX!
?

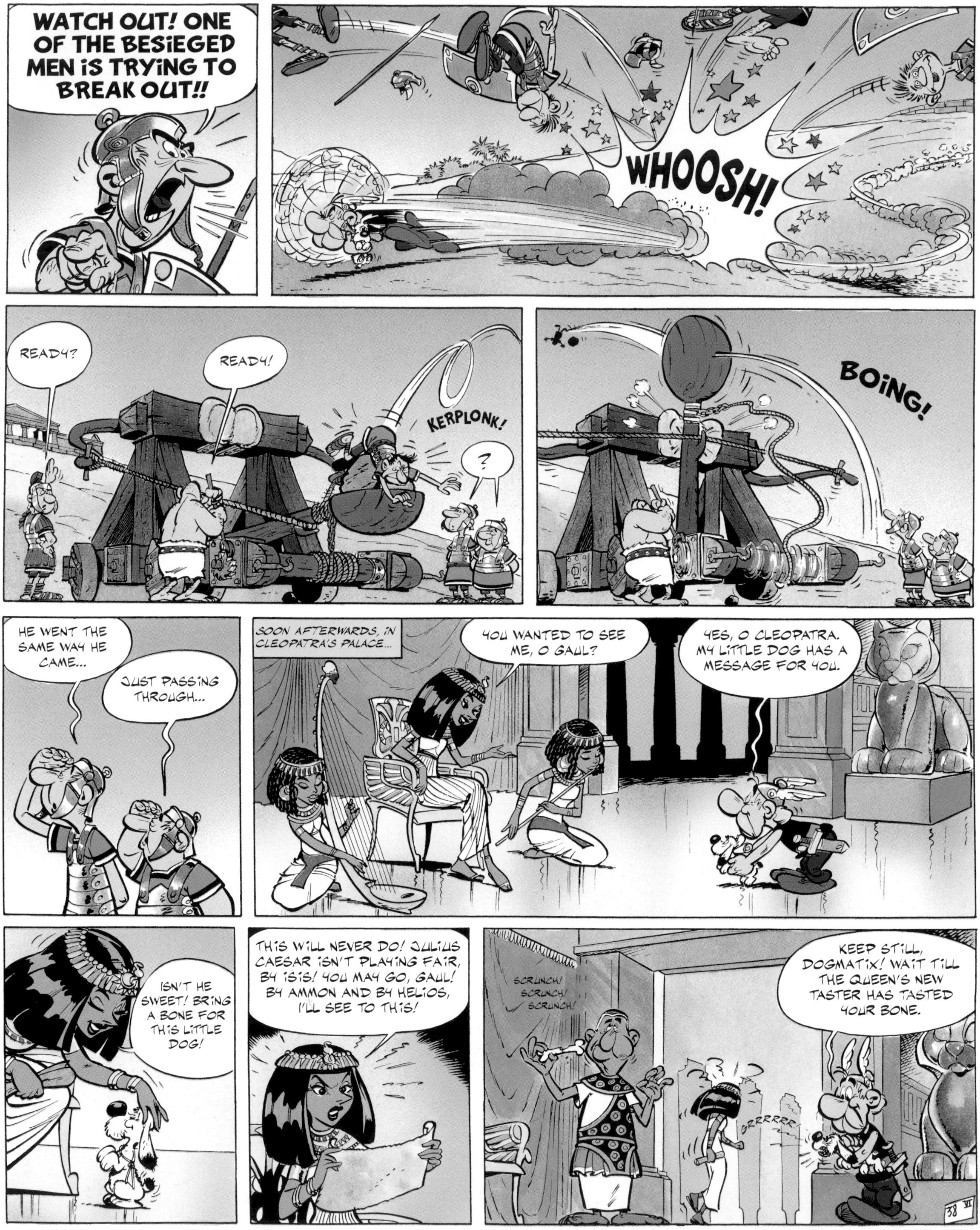
WATCH OUT! ONE OF THE BESIEGED MEN IS TRYING TO BREAK OUT!!
WHOOSH!
READY?
READY!
KERPLONK!
?
BOING!
HE WENT THE SAME WAY HE CAME...
JUST PASSING THROUGH...
SOON AFTERWARDS, IN CLEOPATRA'S PALACE...
YOU WANTED TO SEE ME, O GAUL?
YES, O CLEOPATRA. MY LITTLE DOG HAS A MESSAGE FOR YOU.
ISN'T HE SWEET! BRING A BONE FOR THIS LITTLE DOG!
THIS WILL NEVER DO! JULIUS CAESAR ISN'T PLAYING FAIR, BY ISIS! YOU MAY GO, GAUL! BY AMMON AND BY HELIOS, I'LL SEE TO THIS!
SCRUNCH! SCRUNCH! SCRUNCH!
GRRRRRR!
KEEP STILL, DOGMATIX! WAIT TILL THE QUEEN'S NEW TASTER HAS TASTED YOUR BONE.

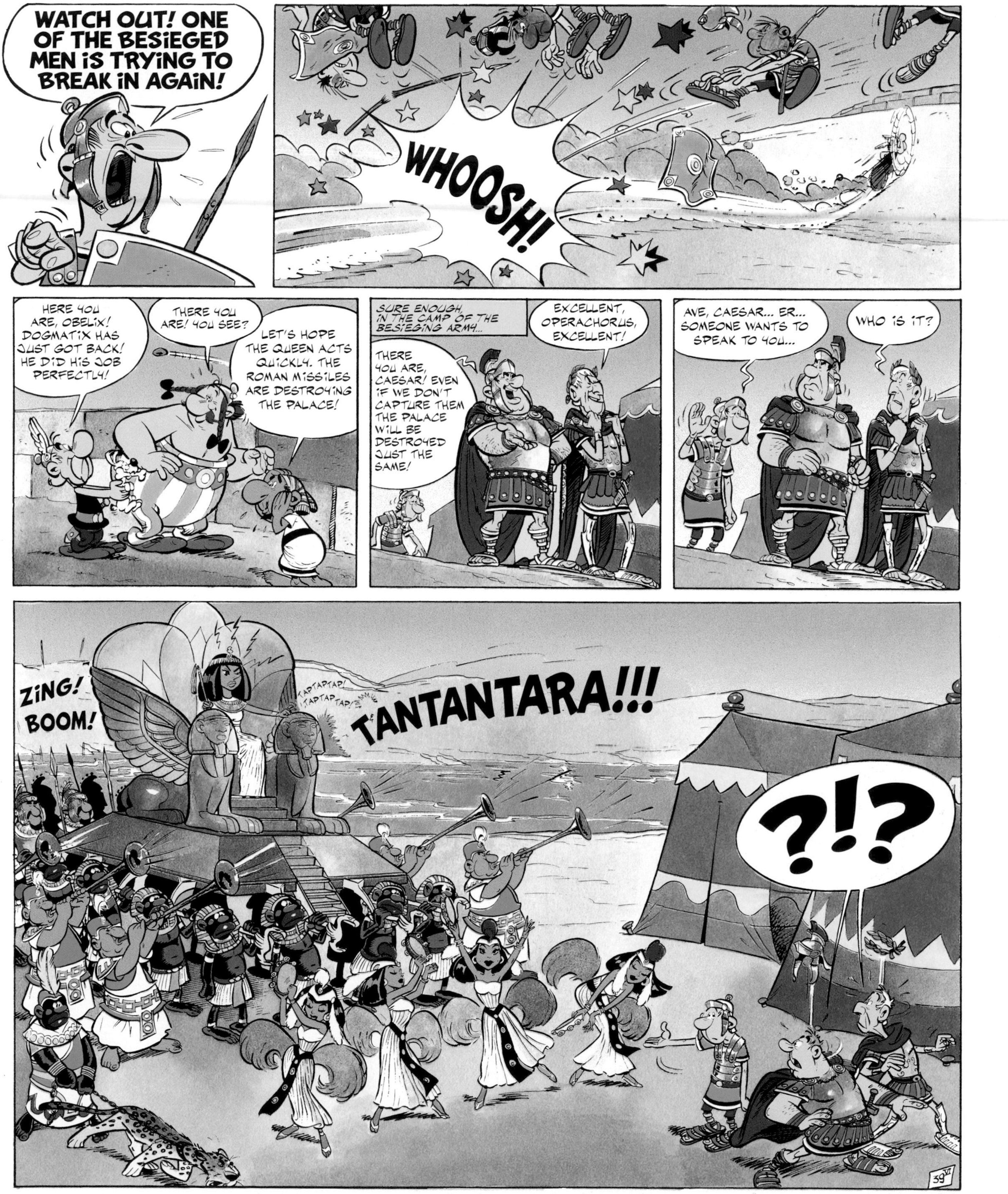

WATCH OUT! ONE OF THE BESIEGED MEN IS TRYING TO BREAK IN AGAIN!
WHOOSH!
HERE YOU ARE, OBELIX! DOGMATIX HAS JUST GOT BACK! HE DID HIS JOB PERFECTLY!
THERE YOU ARE! YOU SEE?
LET'S HOPE THE QUEEN ACTS QUICKLY. THE ROMAN MISSILES ARE DESTROYING THE PALACE!
SURE ENOUGH, IN THE CAMP OF THE BESIEGING ARMY...
THERE YOU ARE, CAESAR! EVEN IF WE DON'T CAPTURE THEM THE PALACE WILL BE DESTROYED JUST THE SAME!
EXCELLENT, OPERACHORUS, EXCELLENT!
AVE, CAESAR... ER... SOMEONE WANTS TO SPEAK TO YOU...
WHO IS IT?
ZING!
BOOM!
TANTANTARA!!!
?!?

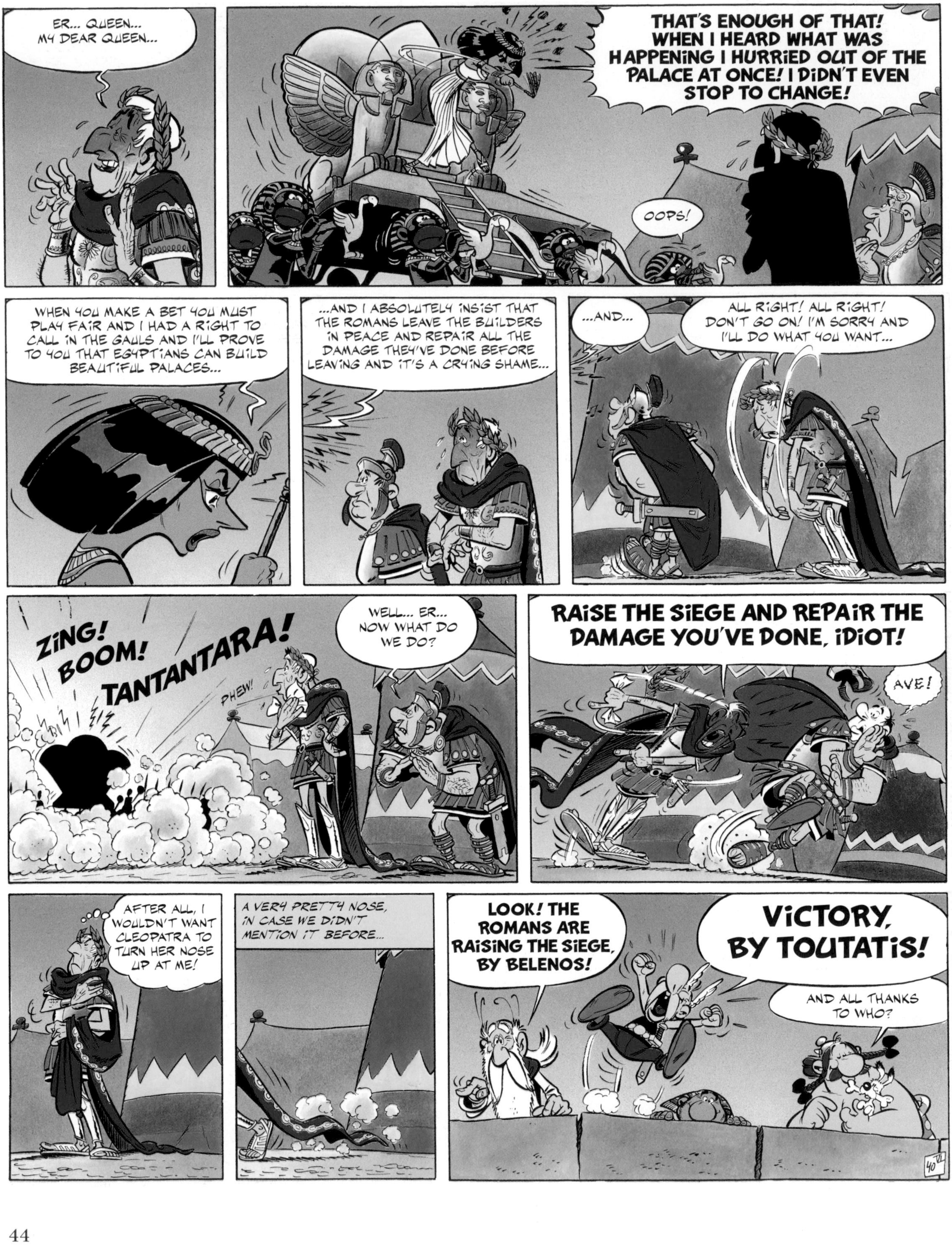
ER... QUEEN... MY DEAR QUEEN...
THAT'S ENOUGH OF THAT! WHEN I HEARD WHAT WAS HAPPENING I HURRIED OUT OF THE PALACE AT ONCE! I DIDN'T EVEN STOP TO CHANGE!
OOPS!
WHEN YOU MAKE A BET YOU MUST PLAY FAIR AND I HAD A RIGHT TO CALL IN THE GAULS AND I'LL PROVE TO YOU THAT EGYPTIANS CAN BUILD BEAUTIFUL PALACES...
...AND I ABSOLUTELY INSIST THAT THE ROMANS LEAVE THE BUILDERS IN PEACE AND REPAIR ALL THE DAMAGE THEY'VE DONE BEFORE LEAVING AND IT'S A CRYING SHAME...
...AND...
ALL RIGHT! ALL RIGHT! DON'T GO ON! I'M SORRY AND I'LL DO WHAT YOU WANT...
ZING! BOOM! TANTANTARA!
PHEW!
WELL... ER... NOW WHAT DO WE DO?
RAISE THE SIEGE AND REPAIR THE DAMAGE YOU'VE DONE, IDIOT!
AVE!
AFTER ALL, I WOULDN'T WANT CLEOPATRA TO TURN HER NOSE UP AT ME!
A VERY PRETTY NOSE, IN CASE WE DIDN'T MENTION IT BEFORE...
LOOK! THE ROMANS ARE RAISING THE SIEGE, BY BELENOS!
VICTORY, BY TOUTATIS!
AND ALL THANKS TO WHO?
40

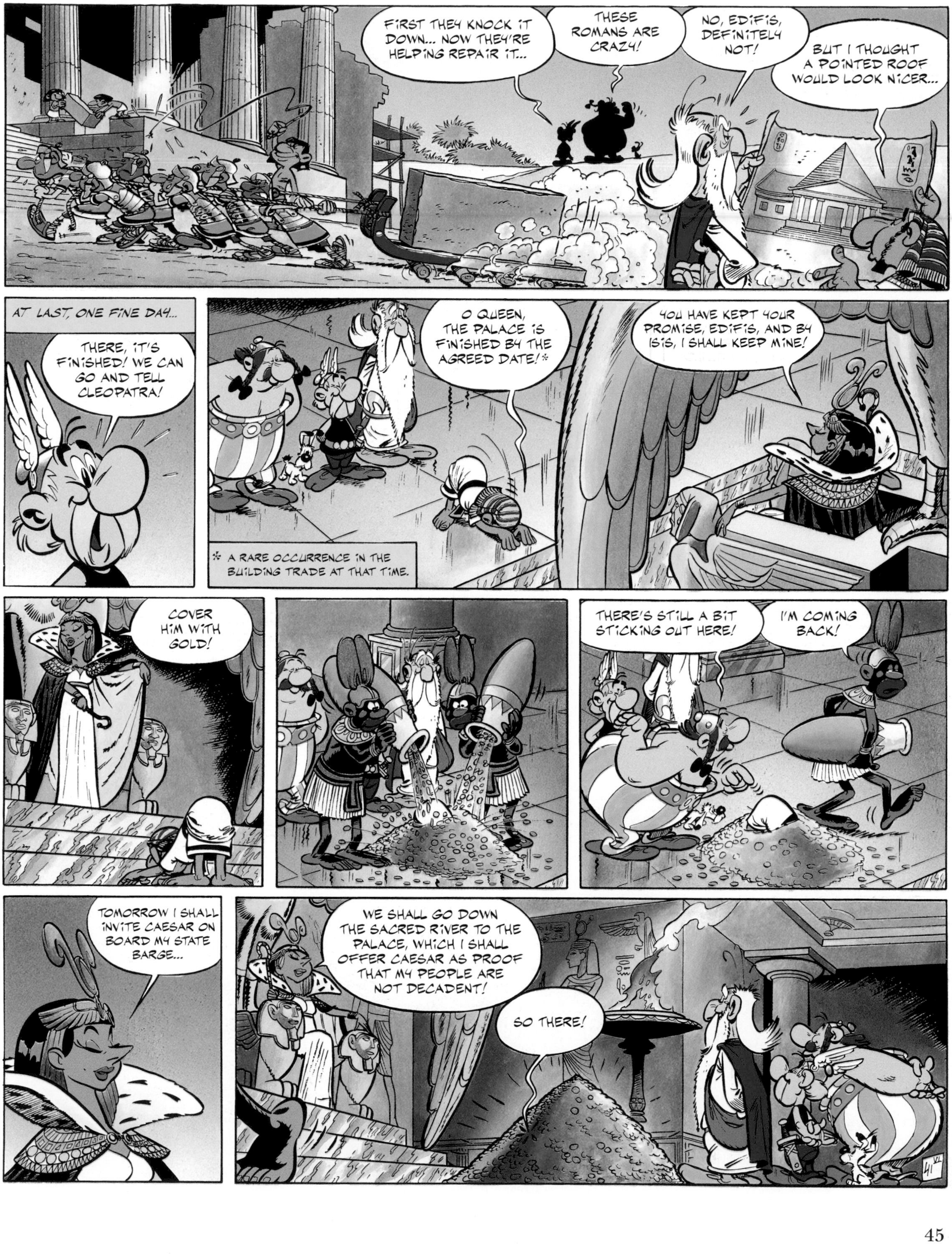
FIRST THEY KNOCK IT DOWN... NOW THEY'RE HELPING REPAIR IT...
THESE ROMANS ARE CRAZY!
NO, EDIFIS, DEFINITELY NOT!
BUT I THOUGHT A POINTED ROOF WOULD LOOK NICER...
AT LAST, ONE FINE DAY...
THERE, IT'S FINISHED! WE CAN GO AND TELL CLEOPATRA!
O QUEEN, THE PALACE IS FINISHED BY THE AGREED DATE!*
* A RARE OCCURRENCE IN THE BUILDING TRADE AT THAT TIME.
YOU HAVE KEPT YOUR PROMISE, EDIFIS, AND BY ISIS, I SHALL KEEP MINE!
COVER HIM WITH GOLD!
THERE'S STILL A BIT STICKING OUT HERE!
I'M COMING BACK!
TOMORROW I SHALL INVITE CAESAR ON BOARD MY STATE BARGE...
WE SHALL GO DOWN THE SACRED RIVER TO THE PALACE, WHICH I SHALL OFFER CAESAR AS PROOF THAT MY PEOPLE ARE NOT DECADENT!
SO THERE!

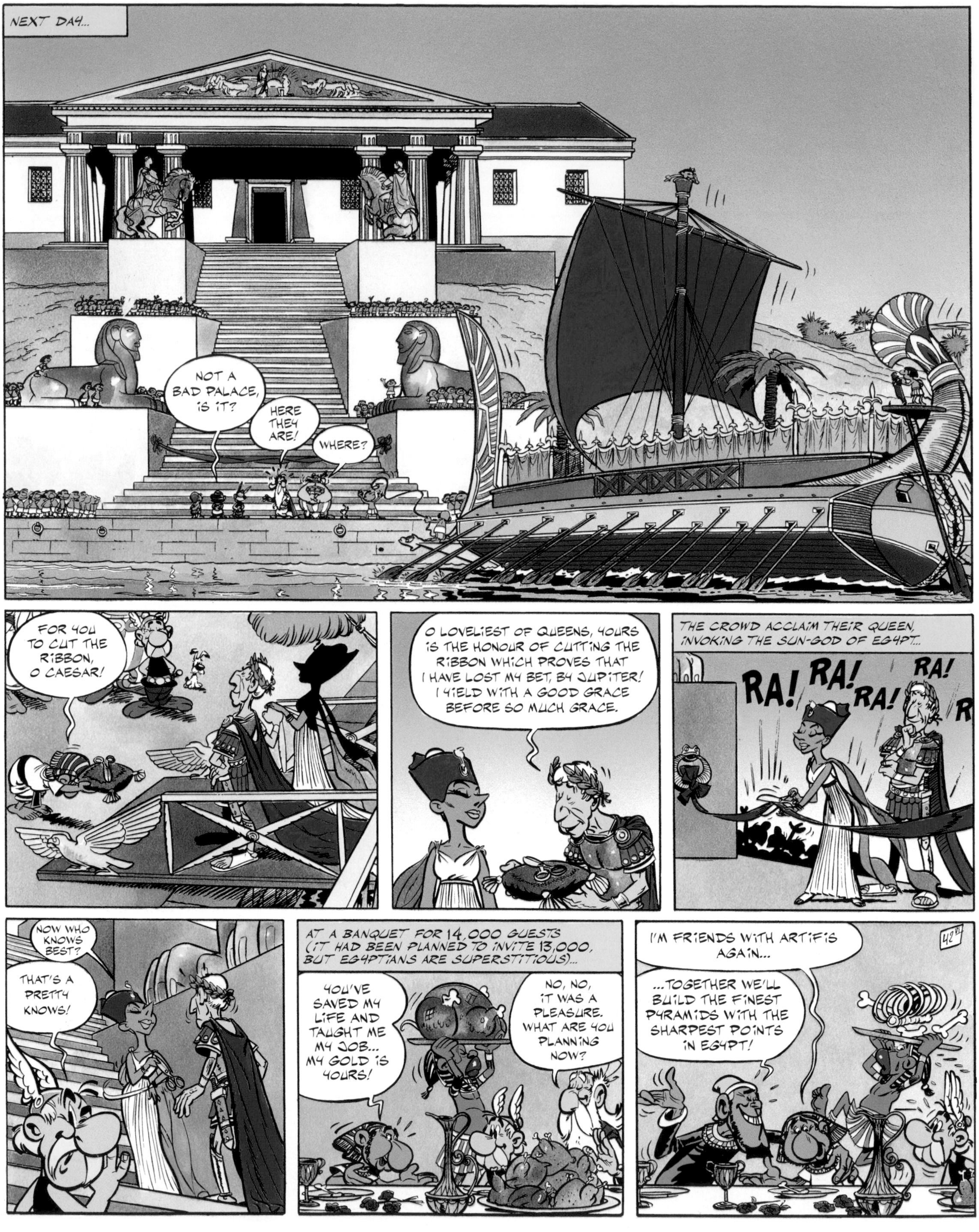
NEXT DAY...
NOT A BAD PALACE, IS IT?
HERE THEY ARE!
WHERE?
FOR YOU TO CUT THE RIBBON, O CAESAR!
O LOVELIEST OF QUEENS, YOURS IS THE HONOUR OF CUTTING THE RIBBON WHICH PROVES THAT I HAVE LOST MY BET, BY JUPITER! I YIELD WITH A GOOD GRACE BEFORE SO MUCH GRACE.
THE CROWD ACCLAIM THEIR QUEEN, INVOKING THE SUN-GOD OF EGYPT...
RA! RA! RA! RA!
NOW WHO KNOWS BEST?
THAT'S A PRETTY KNOWS!
AT A BANQUET FOR 14,000 GUESTS (IT HAD BEEN PLANNED TO INVITE 13,000, BUT EGYPTIANS ARE SUPERSTITIOUS)...
YOU'VE SAVED MY LIFE AND TAUGHT ME MY JOB... MY GOLD IS YOURS!
NO, NO, IT WAS A PLEASURE. WHAT ARE YOU PLANNING NOW?
I'M FRIENDS WITH ARTIFIS AGAIN...
...TOGETHER WE'LL BUILD THE FINEST PYRAMIDS WITH THE SHARPEST POINTS IN EGYPT!

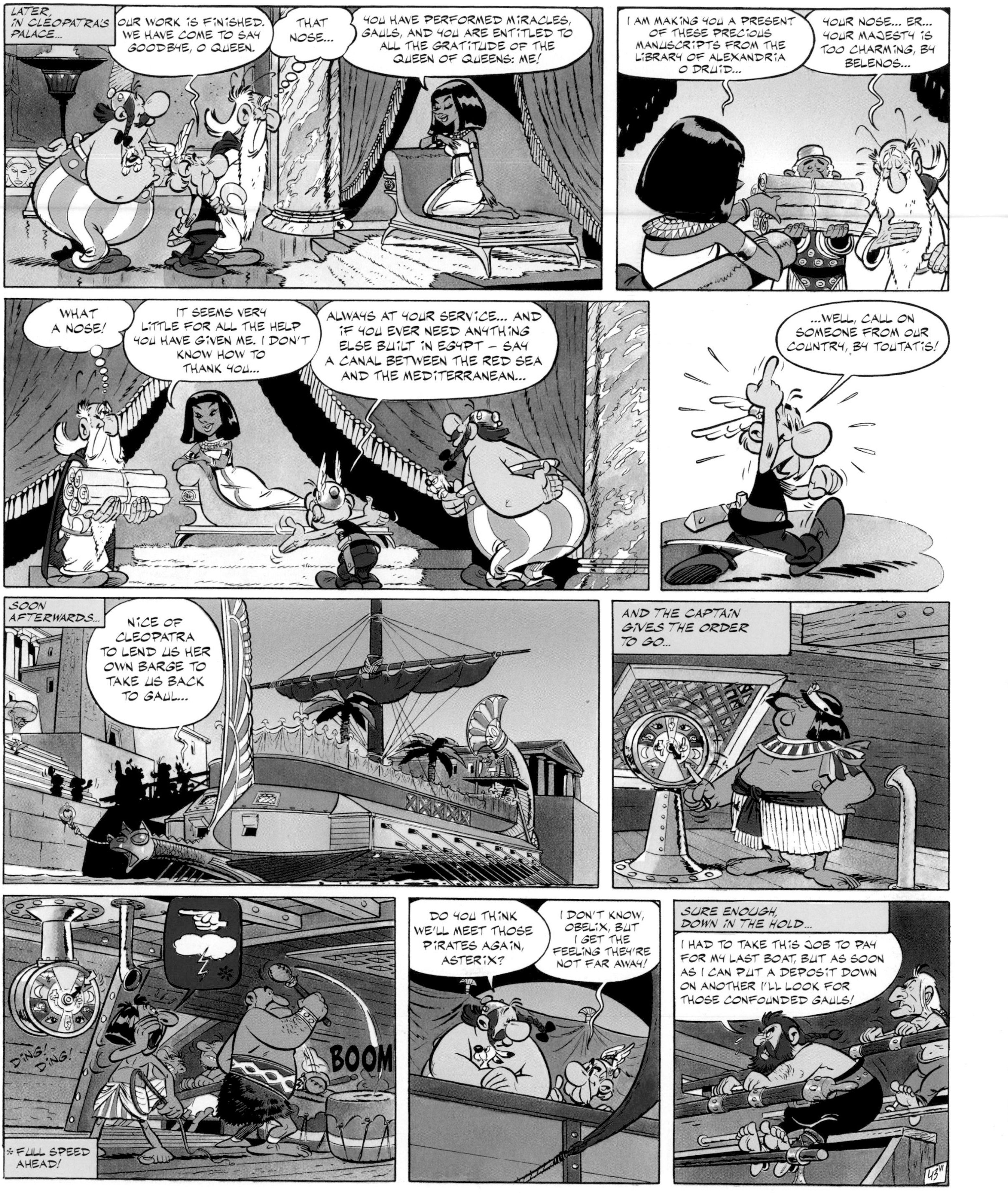
LATER, IN CLÉOPATRA'S PALACE...
OUR WORK IS FINISHED. WE HAVE COME TO SAY GOODBYE, O QUEEN.
THAT NOSE...
YOU HAVE PERFORMED MIRACLES, GAULS, AND YOU ARE ENTITLED TO ALL THE GRATITUDE OF THE QUEEN OF QUEENS: ME!
I AM MAKING YOU A PRESENT OF THESE PRECIOUS MANUSCRIPTS FROM THE LIBRARY OF ALEXANDRIA O DRUID...
YOUR NOSE... ER... YOUR MAJESTY IS TOO CHARMING, BY BELENOS...
WHAT A NOSE!
IT SEEMS VERY LITTLE FOR ALL THE HELP YOU HAVE GIVEN ME. I DON'T KNOW HOW TO THANK YOU...
ALWAYS AT YOUR SERVICE... AND IF YOU EVER NEED ANYTHING ELSE BUILT IN EGYPT – SAY A CANAL BETWEEN THE RED SEA AND THE MEDITERRANEAN...
...WELL, CALL ON SOMEONE FROM OUR COUNTRY, BY TOUTATIS!
SOON AFTERWARDS...
NICE OF CLEOPATRA TO LEND US HER OWN BARGE TO TAKE US BACK TO GAUL...
AND THE CAPTAIN GIVES THE ORDER TO GO...
DING! DING!
BOOM
* FULL SPEED AHEAD!
DO YOU THINK WE'LL MEET THOSE PIRATES AGAIN, ASTERIX?
I DON'T KNOW, OBELIX, BUT I GET THE FEELING THEY'RE NOT FAR AWAY!
SURE ENOUGH, DOWN IN THE HOLD...
I HAD TO TAKE THIS JOB TO PAY FOR MY LAST BOAT, BUT AS SOON AS I CAN PUT A DEPOSIT DOWN ON ANOTHER I'LL LOOK FOR THOSE CONFOUNDED GAULS!

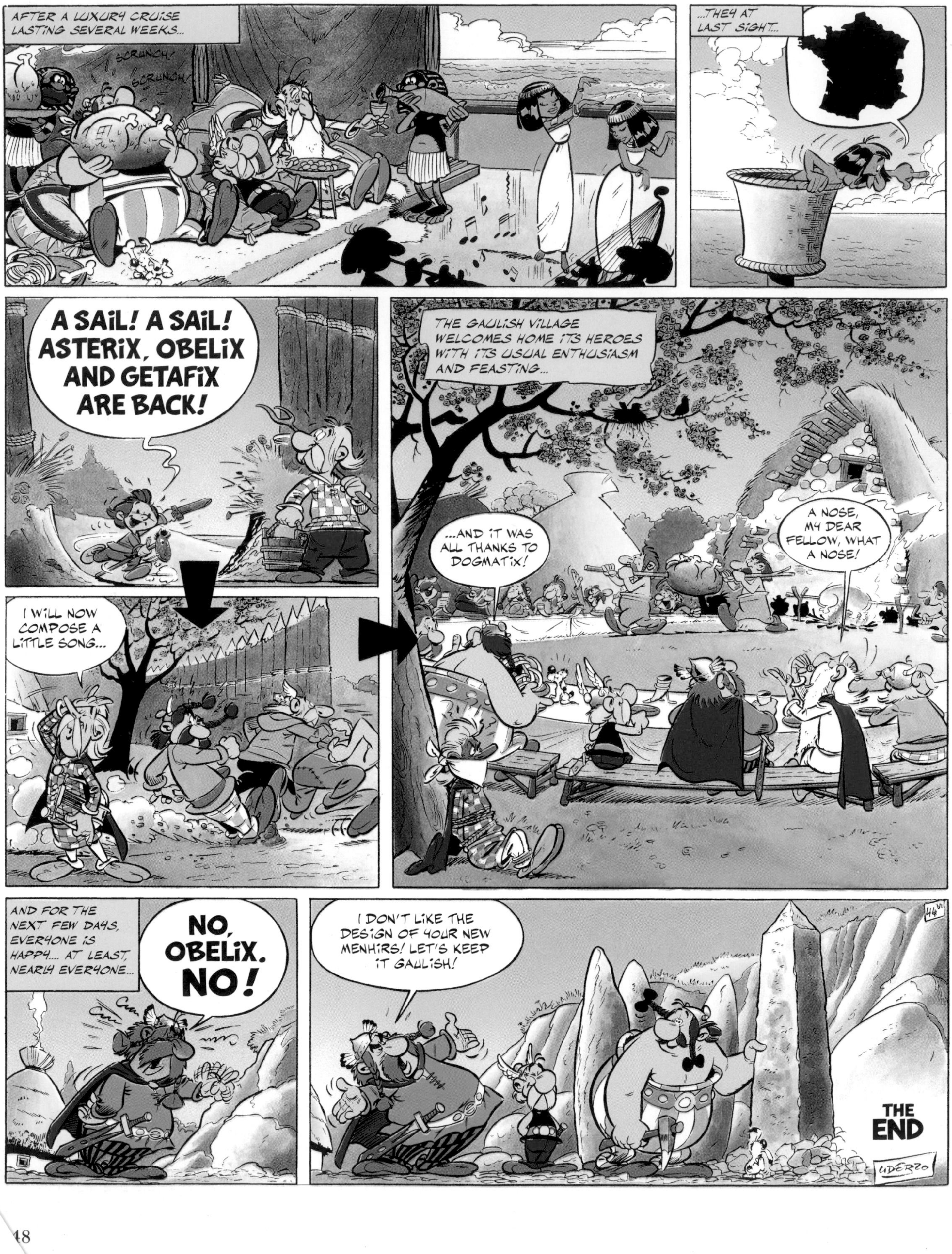

AFTER A LUXURY CRUISE LASTING SEVERAL WEEKS...
SCRUNCH! SCRUNCH!
...THEY AT LAST SIGHT...
A SAIL! A SAIL! ASTERIX, OBELIX AND GETAFIX ARE BACK!
I WILL NOW COMPOSE A LITTLE SONG...
THE GAULISH VILLAGE WELCOMES HOME ITS HEROES WITH ITS USUAL ENTHUSIASM AND FEASTING...
...AND IT WAS ALL THANKS TO DOGMATIX!
A NOSE, MY DEAR FELLOW, WHAT A NOSE!
AND FOR THE NEXT FEW DAYS, EVERYONE IS HAPPY... AT LEAST, NEARLY EVERYONE...
NO, OBELIX. NO!
I DON'T LIKE THE DESIGN OF YOUR NEW MENHIRS! LET'S KEEP IT GAULISH!
THE END
UDERZO